Haunted in Hollywood

the Adventures of Loey Lane

xox

Haunted in Hollywood

the Adventures of Loey Lane
xox

by Loey Lane
with J.A. Kazimer

SH STYLEHAUL / ADAPTIVE BOOKS

AN IMPRINT OF ADAPTIVE STUDIOS | CULVER CITY, CA

Adaptive Books
3578 Hayden Avenue, Suite 6
Culver City, CA 90232

Visit us on the web at www.adaptivestudios.com

Library of Congress Cataloging-in-Publication Number: 2017952105
ISBN 978-1-945293-32-0
Ebook ISBN 978-1-945293-44-3

Printed in the United States of America.

Designed by Whitney Manger

10 9 8 7 6 5 4 3 2 1

This book is dedicated to all of you. My Lovebugs, my LitSquad, my very best friends. Whether you've been watching my channel from the very beginning or just last week, you are my family and we did this together. Thank you for being part of this and sticking with me on this crazy ride. Can you believe we have a book?

CHAPTER 1

THE HOLLYWOOD ROOSEVELT Hotel stood tall against the smoggy LA sunshine, the red-lit sign above acting like a beacon for tourists and stars alike. Palm trees surrounded it, shading the Hollywood elite who sauntered through the doors. The richer and more famous a star, the deeper the saunter.

I tried not to appear too starstruck, fitting the small-town-girl-in-the-big-city cliché, but it was hard when I caught sight of Chris Pine and Brody Jenner heading inside for an afternoon lunch at the burger joint, 25 Degrees.

A part of me suddenly felt like an interloper. I didn't belong here. As soon as that thought rushed through my head, I pushed it back to whatever stupid place it had come from. I belonged here as much as the next person.

"OMG, is that really you?" a girl in skinny jeans and a T-shirt exclaimed.

I glanced around, not seeing anyone but me standing on the famous Hollywood Boulevard sidewalk. I plastered on a bright smile. "I guess, if you think I'm Loey Lane and not Kim K."

"I do!" she yelled, showing off slightly crooked teeth lined with silver braces. "I love you so much."

"I love you more," I said, holding my limbs wide.

The girl rushed into my open arms, hugging me tightly. "I just love your paranormal story times. The last one, about the time you went to Disneyland and saw that spirit . . . I didn't sleep for a week."

"Thank you." I ignored the chill rising on my skin at the memory of my ghostly ride through the *Pirates of the Caribbean*.

"And your bikini videos . . . I love your confidence in your body." She licked her lips. "It's hard . . . sometimes. . . ."

"I know," I said. "But please, know you are beautiful."

Tears shimmered in her eyes. "I do. Because of you and your YouTube channel."

My own eyes grew misty. "You don't know how much that means to me."

"Lana," an older woman with similar features to the girl called from a parked car nearby. "What have I told you about talking to strangers?"

The girl ducked her head, twin red spots staining her cheeks. "Mom," she said in a tone reserved for embarrassed teens everywhere.

I waved at the woman. "It was a pleasure to meet you, Lana," I said to the girl. "Snap or tweet me. I'd love to chat more."

"I will," she said, her smile so wide I thought it might crack her lips. With another quick hug, she headed off to her mother's stern lecture on stranger-danger.

The young girl's words acted as a salve for my silly insecurities. Holding my head high, I did my best imitation of a saunter into the hotel. Hard to do in four-inch heels. But years of practice had prepared me for moments like this.

Walk on your toes, and whatever you do, don't look down.

Or was that when scaling the rope at gym class?

Same principle, I guess. This was a skill every model needed. Or at least, I thought so. I was still learning the modeling ropes, since my career path had recently evolved from vlogger to plus-size fashion model.

Just inside the hotel entrance, I pulled to a stop. The lobby was a study in opulence. Everywhere I looked things sparkled and shined, from the brass accents to the staff itself.

"Can I get your bags?" a bellhop in a gold uniform with brocade accents asked with a welcoming smile. I nodded and he headed outside to get my luggage. I watched through the window as he struggled with my three bags. I winced, knowing I'd overpacked a bit.

As the bellhop hefted each bag, his welcoming smile grew more brittle.

By the final bag, he held the small of his back, grimacing.

I vowed to tip him well.

With a guilty sigh, I headed to the reception desk to check in. A frowning woman in a suit stood behind the polished wood counter, her fingers flying over a keyboard. I cleared my throat to gain her attention. "Loey Lane," I began. "It's like *Zoey* with an *L*."

She blinked a few times, and then smiled, changing her whole appearance. She was actually very pretty under her displeasure. "Are you checking in, or did you just want me to know your name?"

"Checking in, please. I'm a"—I stumbled a bit over the next word—"model with *FAS*, the fashion magazine." A poorly named but very popular magazine for fashion and beauty. I was excited to be a part of its Marilyn Monroe edition. Marilyn was one of my idols. She broke molds in the modeling industry, a true body-positive icon.

"Oh. Of course," she said. Her fingers slid over the keyboard as she made grunting noises. Forehead wrinkling, she finally glanced up from her computer screen. "I am so sorry, but we don't have a room available for you."

"Excuse me?" My stomach churned with anxiety. This couldn't be happening. "The art director booked me a room. I have a confirmation number." I tapped my phone, pulling up the email with the number. I showed it to her. She did some fancy keystroking again.

And for the second time she shook her head. "I'm sorry. . . ."

"This can't be happening," I said. My big break into modeling, an actual cover . . . "Please, do you have any vacancies? I have to stay here. The magazine specifically said so." Which I had thought was an odd request, but it was their dime, so I had agreed.

A mistake, apparently.

"Is there a problem?" a man in a dark suit, his lapel perfectly aligned, asked.

The clerk jumped to attention, her back straight. "This woman says she's with *FAS*, but I can't find a record of her in our system."

"Is that so?" The man derailed her with a look. It wasn't that his frown was anything out of the ordinary, just a regular old downward smile, but the way the woman reacted suggested he might eat puppies for dinner. She twirled on her heel, and disappeared into the back room.

"I am sorry, Miss . . . ?" he said.

"Lane. Loey Lane."

"Unfortunately, we don't have any extra rooms available this week. Big clown convention in town. Who knew large clowns were a thing?" He paused, his eyes on mine. "May I make a suggestion?"

I nodded. "Please."

"*FAS* rented out bungalow space for their original cover model."

"Original cover model?"

"Apparently she took off with a production assistant right before the shoot started." He stopped, lowering his voice. "Big uproar about it."

"Oh." I tried not to stress about filling the shoes of another model. Though this could launch my modeling career.

"Anyway," he said, "perhaps you could stay in that room?" He quickly went on when I failed to look convinced. "It's lovely. A poolside bungalow named after Marilyn Monroe. Big enough for an entire family, so even if Ms. Cook returns after her leave of absence, there will be plenty of room."

I frowned. "Ms. Cook? As in Emily Cook?" I knew Emily from her YouTube channel. She vlogged about fashion and modeling. I'd learned plenty about the fashion industry, both good and bad, from her tutorial videos. Why had the magazine wanted me for the cover after Emily left? The only similarity we shared was our age. Emily was tall, with dark hair and a world-weary stare I would never get right. I didn't do boredom. Life was much too full of adventure.

Why did the art director now want me? Had they changed the cover concept? Was that why Emily really had left? A mystery for sure, but one I didn't have time to solve. Not when I very well might be sleeping on a deck chair next to the pool if I didn't agree to the bungalow.

"What do you think?" the gentleman asked.

"Why not?"

"Wonderful," he said. He went behind the desk, typed in a few keystrokes, and then handed me a vintage plastic key card. I was surprised to see it. Most of the places I stayed in LA used mobile apps, but apparently, the Roosevelt opted for old school. Given the options for sleeping on the boulevard or in a nice bungalow, I'd make do with the card. He snapped his fingers, and the bellhop who'd carried my bags in arrived at my side. He gave me a small, pain-riddled smile.

"Please show her to the Marilyn bungalow," the older man said.

With a sigh the bellhop nodded, hefting my bags onto a luggage cart. I followed him through the lobby, toward the sparkling aquamarine waters of the pool and the famed mural painted by pop artist David Hockney at the bottom. The mural was said to give the patron the impression of swimming in the deep waters of the ocean. I loved it at first sight.

It was just the sort of thing that screamed LA.

I could hardly contain my excitement. Literally. I let out a squeal of delight when we arrived at the bungalow. A bungalow big enough to fit a rather large extended family.

Maybe even my entire LitSquad.

I pulled out my iPhone to capture the beauty surrounding me for my vlog. No filter needed; the room stunned on its own. A large painting of Marilyn stood over a marble fireplace, oddly reminding me of Monet's water lilies in its beauty, but with far less insanity.

The image of Monroe was black-and-white with a dash of red lipstick. The rest of the bungalow followed a similar black-and-white color scheme. Or would that be a lack of color scheme? Either way, the place was a thing of beauty. I couldn't wait to dive into the super-tall white silk sheets.

The bellhop showed me around the room and the various hiding places and secret nooks for amenities and electronics alike. The TV was behind a wall that moved up and down like a curtain when I pressed a button on the remote. The lights worked off the same remote. There was even a telephone in the restroom. Not as exciting as it was pre–cell phone days, but still. . . .

"Do you need anything else, Ms. Lane?" the bellhop asked, his hands behind his back.

"No, thank you. Hold on while I get you a tip." I set my phone down on the bed, digging around in my bag until I grasped the cool leather of my wallet. I counted out a fat tip before passing it to the bellhop. He smiled gratefully and then left, closing the door behind him.

I twirled around, happy to be surrounded by luxury and the hazy California sun. I wanted to slip into my newest bikini, a brilliant black with red cherries strategically placed, and head out to the pool, but I had work to do first.

I dragged one of the suitcases, inch by inch, to the bathroom, where I started to set up shop. I neatly laid out my makeup in order of importance. Concealer for under the eyes, since I rarely slept a full six hours a night, always came first. I would die—literally—without it. Mascara soon followed, as did a wealth of other beauty supplies. Finally my beloved curling iron. Give me liberty or give me death, but don't you dare take away my curls.

I glanced at my iPhone. Much to my surprise, over an hour had already passed.

Once I was done with the bathroom, I moved to the larger bedroom off to the right to put away my clothes. The overly large, fluffy bed beckoned. It just begged to be jumped on. But I was an adult now. Twenty-one and counting.

I glanced to the left and then the right.

Who was I kidding? Seconds later, I was bouncing up and down, snorting with laughter.

After my bounce, I opened the closet door to hang my suitcase-wrinkled clothes, and was shocked to find it filled with dresses. I frowned. Was this Emily's wardrobe? A set of pink leather bags sat on the floor.

I lifted one in particular, swallowing hard.

The air around me suddenly grew ice-cold.

So cold my breath came out in a vapor cloud.

A shiver ran through me as a pink haze filled my vision.

Just as quickly, the room warmed again and the fog vanished.

But that didn't change the very real fact: something was very wrong.

Whatever had happened to Emily Cook, one thing was certain: she hadn't left of her own accord. For if I'd learned one lesson from her channel, I knew no model in her right mind would take off without her makeup—the makeup filling the pink toiletry case in my hand.

CHAPTER 2

AFTER THE UNSHAKABLE feeling Emily Cook hadn't run off with a production assistant as rumored, I put a call in to the art director, to discuss what I found, but the phone rang unanswered.

Odd, considering everyone these days has a phone affixed to their ears.

I debated what to do next.

Until the art director returned my call, I might as well make use of the warming UV rays as well as the cooling blue water of the pool. After I claimed a poolside lounger, I slathered on sunscreen, SPF 7,000,000.

Much to my surprise, a man in a white suit—normally reserved for proms, weddings, and long days at tropical resorts—gave me a small wave. He was older, maybe in his thirties, his hair already slightly receding, but handsome nonetheless. A group of beyond-beautiful women stood around him, sipping at fancy cocktails in their hands.

Actresses or models—I was nearly sure of it.

"Loey! Girl, you look amazing." The man came forward as if we'd known each other for all of our lives. In truth, while he looked vaguely familiar, I couldn't remember ever having met him before.

When I noticed the camera in his hand, it clicked.

I was standing in the path of fashion-magazine greatness. Jean-Claude Petit, the famed photographer in front of me, had shot some of the most beautiful women on the planet in his career. His photographs had once graced the covers of *Vogue*, *Elle*, and *GQ*.

I hadn't met him, not in person at least. Though I followed his career when I was younger. I hadn't seen any covers by him in recent memory. I'd heard rumors, though. Whispered warnings for inexperienced models like myself. He'd developed quite the reputation for taking too many liberties on past shoots. I didn't know if the claims were true. I hoped not. Even if they were, people changed. Maybe he'd be the perfect gentleman all shoot.

He moved in, air kissing both of my cheeks. He smelled of overpowering cologne and mints. "Aren't you divine in that bikini."

"Thank you," I said. "I can't wait to start shooting. Tomorrow, right?"

"Yes." He motioned to the diving board at the head of the pool. "We'll begin there. Right where Marilyn did her first shoot."

I smiled, picturing the famed photograph of Marilyn Monroe, barely nineteen years old, leaning back on the diving board, her head thrown back as if laughing at the world. According to the art director who hired me, *FAS* wanted to re-create her shoot for the cover, along with some interior fashion shots around the hotel. The concept thrilled me. I began to blather about just how much.

His lips curved into a smirk at my eagerness. "We can go into details tomorrow, but for now, I want to introduce you to my assistants and your fellow models along for this fabulous ride."

"I'd love that," I said. This was a perfect chance to learn more about the business. A vlog and a few local catalog gigs hadn't prepared me for a cover shoot. I felt very much like a fish out of water.

"Ethan! Roger!" he yelled. "Come meet the beauty who is saving our collective bacon."

I licked my suddenly dry lips. "I don't think that's quite true, but thank you for saying so."

Jean-Claude snorted. "Don't be silly. Without you we wouldn't have a shoot, since Emily pulled her typical disappearing act."

Nothing seemed typical about leaving a cover shoot without one's makeup case. I began to say as much. "Speaking of Emily, I found her luggage along with a makeup kit in the bungalow."

"Toss it," he said with a growl. "If she thinks she can do better . . ."

Before he could finish his statement, two men appeared in front of us. If not for the different-colored drinks in their hands, I would've had a hard time distinguishing between them. Both were tall and blond and wore perfectly pressed, fashionable matching outfits and mandatory black-rimmed eyeglasses.

"These are my assistants," Jean-Claude said.

The one with the blue drink, Roger, kissed my hand, squealing with delight as he declared his love of me and my YouTube channel. "I adore your story times. And that story about your crazy ex-roommate—I just . . . OMG."

I tried not to blush. It amazed me every time someone gushed over my channel, let alone me. It felt alien. To me, and to most of my friends and family, I was a midwestern girl. I did my laundry at the laundromat, shopped at the local Target, and watched Netflix on most Friday nights.

It amazed me daily: a channel born from a lonely teenager had taken on a life all its own. I loved every minute of the ride, wherever it might take me. For example, poolside at the famed Hollywood Roosevelt Hotel, about to shoot my very first cover, let alone a cover for a national magazine. It all felt surreal.

After Roger released my hand, the second assistant stepped forward.

Ethan, the assistant with a pink drink cupped in his hand, was more reserved in his greeting than the first, but just as kind. Not to mention his midwestern twang that instantly set me at ease. "It's good to meet you. I look forward to working together."

Maybe I'd fit in just fine.

A thought that persisted up until I met the first of the models.

"June." Jean-Claude motioned an asymmetrical, pony-haired woman my way. She wore a white bikini; her skin glistened with sunscreen. "I want you to meet someone special," he said to her. "This is Loey Lane." He smiled at me. "If you'll excuse me, I need to check on something. Please, talk. Get to know each other." With that, he walked away to do whatever needed to be done.

"It's nice to meet you," I said.

Her uninterested gaze flickered over me.

I tried to engage her again. "I have to admit, I'm a little nervous about the shoot."

She glanced over my shoulder as if looking for someone. "Do you live here?"

Now her eyes found mine. "At the hotel? No."

Once again, her eyes sought more interesting conversational partners.

I gave a small laugh. "I meant in LA." When I didn't get a response, I said, "I live in Manhattan."

At the name of the celebrated East Coast city, she focused on me and for the first time looked attentive.

I winced, correcting the implication. "Manhattan, Kansas. Not New York."

Before I could start another sentence, she turned on her six-inch white stiletto heel and left to talk to a group of businessmen drinking expensive vodka at the bar. I tried not to take her leaving personally, but it sparked the insecurities buried deep nonetheless.

Maybe I didn't belong here after all.

As soon as the thought came, I smashed it back down. Whether or not I belonged, I was here, and I'd do the best job I could. I pulled back my shoulders and held my head high. Keeping it up, I strolled around the pool.

Groups of two or three models were gathered around, each holding a drink, but not a plate of food in sight. I joined the first group, waiting for a good time to introduce myself. Once I did, their reactions varied from disdain to outright annoyance.

Again, I tried not to let their rejection bother me.

I simply headed for the next group. Before I reached them, I overheard loud whispers from the last pairing. One of the models muttered, "Marilyn would be rolling in her grave if she knew they had this YouTube tart playing her."

The other model said, "I bet she's Jean-Claude's side piece."

The first snorted. "I guess he *did* find a replacement for Emily. Lucky girl."

They broke into giggles.

Embarrassment burned my cheeks, and tears pricked the back of my eyes. I'd be damned if I let them fall. The models could think what they wanted.

Unable to face yet another rejection from the mean models, I opted to chat with the most important person poolside. The bartender, Jed. We talked about the famous people he'd met over his long career slinging drinks at the hotel, as well as his love of the LA Dodgers.

An hour later, head swimming, I switched from the lovely, tall, fruity, alcohol-infused drink with a multicolored umbrella that Jed had created—called a Pina Sunrise—to water. One of the models, a young, fresh-faced girl, approached the bar, and leaning on her elbow, she pushed an empty glass toward Jed.

"The same?" he asked.

"Yes, please."

He started to fill her glass, pausing when she asked, "Is the rumor true?"

He leaned in so as not to be overheard. I'll admit, the word *rumor* had peaked my interest, so I bent in as well. "What do you think?" he asked.

"I . . . don't . . . ," she muttered.

Jed looked at me. "What about you, Loey? Do you believe the Roosevelt is haunted?"

I swallowed.

Without waiting for my answer he said, "They say, *if you see her, you'll be the next to die.*"

Before I could freak out, Jed gave me a small wink. I stifled a laugh. When you serve drink after drink to out-of-town guests and LA elite, you have to get your kicks where you can. And this poor young model's reaction was priceless.

"I knew it!" she shouted. "June said I was being ridiculous."

Jed piled on: "I'd sleep with one eye open."

The girl frowned. "But then I'll see her. I don't want to die."

I laughed. "Good point."

She glanced my way, as if noticing me for the first time. "Oh, hi," she said in a surprisingly friendly tone, given my recent rejections by the other models. "I'm Stephi."

"Loey," I responded.

"You're Emily's replacement."

"So they tell me." I smiled at the girl. "Do you know Emily well?"

She shook her head. "Not really. Jean-Claude kept her pretty much to himself, except on the shoot."

As much as I didn't want to gossip, Emily's makeup case increasingly bothered me. "Are he and Emily a pair?"

She shrugged, blowing a bubble with the gum in her mouth. "Not according to Emily, but—"

As if he had a sixth sense, Jean-Claude appeared at my elbow, empty drink in hand. Stephi instantly shut up, and practically ran away, her tonic water on ice forgotten. "Are you enjoying yourself, Loey, luv?" He squeezed my arm, his breath reeking of booze. Not waiting for my answer, he held up his glass, rattling the ice cubes. "Another," he said to Jed.

After Jed refilled his glass, Jean-Claude whispered in my ear. "You are very beautiful. What do you say—"

Awkward.

I jumped up, thankful for my cell phone's perfect timing. "Sorry," I said to him. "I have to get this." Pressing "talk," I answered the call without even glancing at the caller ID.

At that moment, it could have been Jack the Ripper and I would've answered.

"Loey," a voice on the other end said.

I recognized it instantly. "Chase! How are you?" I asked one of my close friends. He lived here in LA, and I hoped I could tear him away from his lavish lifestyle in order to do some sightseeing. We'd met two years ago at a meet-up for YouTube personalities in Santa Monica. Admittedly, Chase and I won Best-Dressed Personalities hands down. Though his Gucci embroidered bomber jacket, fresh off the factory line, had cost three times the price of my entire outfit, including my Christian Louboutin's Venenana ankle-tie sandals. Sure, they were a size too small, but I loved them like no other.

Chase and I chatted for a few minutes as I slipped farther and farther from the now slobby, drunken photographer groping the pony-haired model, June. I tried not to feel sorry for her, but the bored look had disappeared from her face and she now looked positively outraged.

She clutched the lapel of his white suit. "I won't be your second choice."

"It wasn't like—"

"Liar," she hissed, tossing her drink in his face.

Jean-Claude reeled back, his heel teetering on the edge of the pool. As if in slow motion, his drunken state, along with gravity, pulled him over the edge. Water splashed up as he dropped, soaking the meaner models standing poolside.

Nervous laughter ensued.

"Man down," Jed yelled into the house phone.

"I have to go," I said to Chase as I slithered into the bungalow, wanting to avoid whatever altercation happened next. It was late, and I was tired after traveling all day. The cool sheets beckoned as the UV rays had hours ago.

I dropped onto the bed, and my gaze wandered to the closet and the makeup bag tucked inside. I wondered again what had truly happened to Emily Cook.

The room grew cold.

I hugged the comforter around me, debating whether to get out of the warm blanket to turn off the air conditioner. As soon as I started from the bed, the temperature warmed again. Under the steady stream of heated air, my eyes grew heavy, and I leaned back against the headboard.

If you see her . . .

Jed's words flickered through my mind.

I laughed at my own fancy. Ghosts, whether real or not, weren't lying in wait to attack the living. Let alone dying to kill. With a shake of my head at the notion, I turned off the light and slowly drifted off.

CHAPTER 3

SOMETIME LATER, I jolted awake, my heart slamming wildly in my chest. *What is going on?* I took a deep breath. A rush of adrenaline spiked through my body as I recalled just what had startled me.

I'd heard a scream.

I was nearly sure of it. A woman's scream. Loud, high-pitched. Terrified.

Was it a dream?

I didn't think so.

Goose bumps puckered along my skin even in the now-sweltering room.

I quickly leapt from the softness of the bed and flipped on the lights as I threw on one of the hotel robes. The monogrammed kind that they used extra fabric softener on. The room looked the same as when I'd first fallen asleep. No screaming woman hiding in the corner.

At least one I could see.

Swallowing the anxiety bubbling inside my stomach, I dismissed the warning and instead focused on searching for the source of the scream.

When nothing appeared out of the ordinary, I exhaled the breath I'd held. Yet for some reason, my heart still pounded in my chest. Unwillingly, my eyes traveled to the front door, the one that exited to the pool area. Was the pool party still happening? Was that the source of the scream?

I glanced at the time on my phone: 4 a.m.

The pool bar had closed two hours ago. I doubted anyone stuck around after the flow of booze stopped. Nervously, I moved toward the door until my hand hovered above the knob.

Don't do it, a little voice in the back of my mind pleaded.

Like a fool, I opened it anyway.

The pool appeared dark, save for one lone white light under the surface of the water by the diving board. I glanced around at the empty deck.

No screaming woman.

Thank God.

I was being ridiculous. If a woman had yelled, someone else would've noticed and come running. I must've dreamt it.

That was what I got for spending too much time in the sun.

Rubbing the chills from my arms, I turned back toward the bungalow—but stopped before I made a full circle. Something flickered at the end of the pool, almost like an electrical storm. An outline of something began to form, only to suddenly wink out.

Seconds later, another figure, this one more substantial and less electrified, materialized. I peered closer. A pink mist swirled around me, slightly obscuring the vision for a few seconds.

I waved the bizarre smoke away.

Now the full outline of a woman floated above the board in a white flowing dress.

I blinked, unsure if what I saw could be real.

The figure remained.

She raised her arm, pointing at me. Her lips moved, but no sound ventured forth.

Could it be? Was this the ghost Jed had teased Stephi about?

If you see her, you'll be the next to die.

The caution flickered through my head. Before I could gather enough breath to scream, the vision winked out like the first one had. Paralyzed with fear, I could only stare into the darkness where the apparitions had appeared. My own mouth opened and closed, but like the second vision's had, no sound emerged.

A few seconds later, when my body started to function again, I yelped and ran into the bungalow, locking the dead bolt behind me. I slouched against the door, processing what I'd just witnessed.

Had I just seen the infamous, murderous ghost?

The thought had me panicking, so I did the only logical thing I could: I rushed to my iPhone and onto Twitter. My thumbs moved frantically across the keypad as I recounted my encounter with a dead woman.

@Loeybug: GHOST. HERE. AT THE HOTEL.
What should I do?
@JackieJ: Lock the door and hide under the covers
@BPaulE: Show us your boobs!
@BeCloe23: R U sure it was a ghost? How much
have you had to drink?

Much too soon, the bright lights of my iPhone faded as my phone's battery died, leaving me in the dark, fumbling for one of my many chargers. After I located one, I plugged my phone in and switched on every light before diving under the silk bedding. My face peeked out as I waited for certain ghostly death. I stayed like that until the first light of dawn appeared in the large floor-to-ceiling windows.

Only then did I laugh at myself, at my wild imagination.

Jed had gotten me with his practical joke. I bet he played it on all the girls. Fake ghost appearance and everything. He and the other hotel employees must've laughed and laughed at my fright.

With a nervous chuckle, I jammed my sleeping mask over my eyes and finally allowed myself to fall into a fitful sleep. I dreamt of scary, surprisingly big clowns, electrical clouds, pink mist, and women in white.

Don't ask me *Why clowns?*

They're just creepy, and in need of serious makeup tips.

CHAPTER 4

A POUNDING WOKE me the next morning. You'd think it would be a pounding in my head, especially after my lack of sleep from bad dreams the night before. But it wasn't.

The pounding was very real, and at my front door.

I staggered from the bed, wrapping the belt of the robe tightly against my waist. I checked my appearance in the mirror, wincing at the dark circles under my eyes. I'd need half a tube of the hangover cream concealer. A miracle product. But I doubted its effectiveness against my current raccoonish look. I yanked open the door as the knocking continued.

"Loey!" V, my oldest and dearest friend, stood in the doorway, her caramel-colored skin glowing in the morning light. "Are you okay?"

"V?" I bit my lip to choke back the relieved tears in my eyes at the sight of my best friend. We hadn't seen each other in person for over three months, though we talked by text or on the phone every day. She was often my rock when things got too crazy. I loved her, even more than my Christian Louboutins. "What are you . . . How did you . . ." I gave up. Instead I wrapped my arms around her, holding tightly. Her skin felt warm and smelled of coconut sunscreen.

"Oh, sweetie," she said, pulling back once our hug subsided. "Everything is okay now. Ryland and Chase are with me."

V, Ryland, and Chase were part of my core LitSquad. I had friends all over the world, but these three loved me unlike any other, and I felt the same for them. I'd known V since grade school. We'd been fast friends since the day we bonded over makeup and boy talk. My friendships with Ryland and Chase were relatively new in comparison. Nonetheless, they were vital to my continued sanity, as well as super fun.

"I was in Vegas when Chase texted me about your tweet from last night." V shoved her way past me. "You do know, there is no scientific evidence that the supernatural exists. No matter what you say in your paranormal story times."

I ignored V's statement. She didn't believe in anything she couldn't see. I, on the other hand, kept an open mind. Science confirmed the existence of new life-forms every day. Why not spirits? "I'm sure it was just the bartender playing a prank," I said, to avoid the same old argument. "She sure looked ghost-like, though."

"I really have missed you," V said with a grin. She glanced around. "Nice digs."

"Right? I can't believe this place." I twirled around. "It's like I went to sleep in Kansas and woke up in Oz."

She laughed at my Kansas joke. As she always did. Even when they weren't funny.

I smiled at her, amazed after all this time at how beautiful she truly was. Yes, her outsides were nicely proportioned, her hair shiny, her eyes dark and mysterious, from a mix of perfect genes. Yet her brain, grown from those genes, was the most stunning part.

V was damn smart. Like Mensa smart.

"You know I'm thrilled to see you," I said, "but what are you doing here?"

"Chase was concerned. You know how he gets." She waved a manicured hand to the door. "He saw your tweets and decided we needed to protect you from this supposed ghost." She smirked. "Chase sent his jet to Vegas, picked me and Ryland up after Ryland's set, and now we're here. He rocked it, BTW."

I wasn't surprised by either Chase's protectiveness or by Ryland "rocking it." Ryland was one of the best DJs in Vegas. His music got people on their feet. Watching it was akin to a religious experience. Though not an ounce of ego showed in his demeanor. He was the most down-to-earth guy I'd met, spending most of his weekdays serving up meals to the homeless who survived on the Las Vegas strip. I helped whenever I found myself in Sin City. The experience was both beautiful and humbling.

That being said, I couldn't help but protest their desire to safeguard me. "I'm not a child, you know."

"I told him as much." Her gaze flickered over my face. "But, Loey, seriously, someone's messing with you, and I'm going to find out who." V wasn't finished. "Besides, isn't it better to have us here?"

It really was.

Prank or not.

"Loey!" Chase ran into the room with his typical frat-boyish wonder, blond hair styled to perfection. He grabbed me around the waist, hoisting me off my feet. I giggled until he released me. "Poor darling," he said in a drawl. "We're here now. Nothing's going to happen to my love." He snapped his fingers. "*#ThisGhostMessedwiththeWrongGirl.*"

I loved Chase, but he could be overwhelming at times with his hashtags. I gave him a smile, my eyes on his unblemished face. Sometimes I thought I spied foundation on his skin. Not that a guy couldn't wear cosmetics. A YouTube boy friend recently became the face of CoverGirl and looked fabulous doing it. "I'm not even sure what I saw last night," I said. "V's right. It very well might've been a prank."

"I hope it was a ghost," Ryland said, coming into the room. Per normal, he looked like a sloppy version of a copper-haired Justin Timberlake. I often wanted to sit him down and gel his hair in place. "Not one that wants you dead, of course. But I'd like to see one"—a grin flickered over his lips—"before I die."

I winced at his jest. "You've heard the rumor about the ghost killing anyone who sees her?"

"Yes, we heard," V said, glancing back at me. "I don't buy a word of it. 'Hauntings' are so easy to fake. Trust me, there's no ghost out to kill you."

Again V was right. Even if it was a ghost I'd seen, why would she want me dead? I was a nice person. I walked around graves, not on them. The dead and I were on good terms.

"Now get dressed so we can get some waffles," Ryland said, patting his flat stomach. "I'm starving. What kind of private jet doesn't have peanuts?" he complained to Chase.

"I'm allergic to nuts," Chase barked. "I get all puffy and red, which doesn't play well on camera." Chase made videos about growing up as a rich kid in Beverly Hills. His subscribers, mostly other frat boys, loved him, obviously. Then again, who wouldn't? He was warm and sweet under his hashtag, frat-bro demeanor, though his vanity did drive me crazy at times. So many more important things were happening in the world, both on screen and off—how could anyone worry about puffy red cheeks on camera? "Plus," I added casually, "you might, I don't know, die from it. Throat closing up, inability to breathe. . . ."

"When you put it that way," he said with a grin.

I rolled my eyes at his attempt to lighten the mood. "Thank you for coming all this way, but I'm fine. For reals. You can go home."

V laughed, husky and deep, like warm chocolate syrup over ice cream. "Sorry, but we're in for the long haul. After all, who would say no to a Hollywood vaycay? Which bedroom are you using? I'll take the other, and the boys"—her eyes flickered over Ryland, her occasional friend with benefits—"can sleep on the couches."

Before "the boys" could protest, V grabbed her duffel bag, which Ryland had carried in, and disappeared into the smaller bedroom. I frowned after her. Chase patted my shoulder. "Look at it this way," he said, running a hand through his blond hair. "The ghost will have to get through me to get to you."

I laughed, despite myself. "Except for one tiny problem."

His forehead scrunched. "What's that?"

"Ghosts can appear anywhere. They won't knock on the door, asking to be let in to kill me."

"Point taken," he said with a grin. "I could sleep in your room. . . ."

I laughed. "Weakest ploy ever. I think I can manage on my own, but thanks for the altruistic offer."

"You know me," he said. "I care."

"Right." I turned back to the bedroom, feeling happy and relieved to have my friends near. Friendship was what made life so sweet. Every day I was thankful for the gift of my squad. No matter what, I could count on my friends, both in-person and virtual, to offer guidance and love.

And waffles.

"I'm going to get dressed," I said, my hands on my hips. "Then I believe someone said something about buying me breakfast?"

CHAPTER 5

AFTER A GOOEY, warm waffle with pine nuts and pecan syrup, along with four iced coffees, I felt almost human. *Almost.* Last night's lack of sleep had taken its toll, but I had a photo shoot this afternoon, so I had to suck it up and put on my big-girl panties.

Both literally and figuratively.

Once I had slipped those essential shoot-day Spanx on, I squeezed myself into a flowing white dress the magazine stylist had sent over. I peeped at the two-sizes-too-small tag and winced.

That explained why I barely got the dress over my hips, even with my body shapers. The dress fit so tightly I had to take shallow breaths. I wondered if Marilyn had to go through this sort of torture. Probably. Men had always and would always design dresses for maximum appeal and not comfort.

Yet when I gazed into the mirror, the gown swirling at my knees, I had to admit the dress looked good. The whiteness brought out the blue-green of my eyes—a rare recessive trait—along with the deep red of my lipstick. My waist looked smaller, and my breasts appeared two times their normal cup size, thanks to Victoria and my secret.

I took a nervous breath and glanced in the mirror one last time.

With nothing left to primp or prep, I was ready.

Before I turned away, the mirror flickered with light. I spun around to see why, but the sun filtering through the windows hadn't changed. It still gave a soft, diffused light. My eyes went back to the mirror as the space around me grew arctic.

I blew out a cloud of condensation.

My heart slammed in my breast. I closed and then opened my eyes, willing whatever was happening to stop, be it a trick of the light or faulty air-conditioning or something more supernatural.

A pink mist, much like the one I'd witnessed last night, swirled around the bottom of the standing cheval full-length mirror, the old-fashioned kind that stood on a swivel.

My own reflection blurred as another image materialized.

The body of the woman from last night and the vaguest outline of her face. Her white dress so much like mine it was hard to tell them apart in the shiny surface. Her lips moved—at least I thought they were her lips—but again, no sound burst forth.

My own mouth had little trouble this time, for I let out a piercing scream loud enough to cause an earthquake along the San Andreas Fault.

The bedroom door flew open, followed by my LitSquad.

The mirror flickered one last time, and the mist, along with the woman, vanished.

"Loey, are you all right?" Ryland yelled.

V, on his heel, screamed, "What is it? What happened?"

"Did you . . . see that?" I stammered.

"What?" V glanced around.

My hand on my chest to still my pounding heart, I said, "I'm pretty sure I just saw the ghost from last night."

"Here?" Chase drew back, his voice tight. "Now?"

I numbly nodded.

"This is getting ridiculous," V said, looking from me to Chase, and then to Ryland. Her look suggested I was on the verge of mental collapse. I tried not to take offense. V was a science gal. She needed verifiable proof of the existence of an afterlife. My seeing an actual ghost fell short in her estimation.

"We should check into a different hotel," Ryland said, ever pragmatic.

"Can't," I said, my fear fading. The ghost, if that's what I had indeed just witnessed, hadn't killed me. Hadn't even attempted to. I had nothing to fear. At least that's what I told myself, again and again until I nearly believed it. "The magazine insisted I stay here," I said. "They even made it a condition in my contract."

"But why?" V asked, her tone laced with suspicion.

I shrugged. "The art director wants me on call at all hours. He said Jean-Claude, the photographer, likes to take spur-of-the-moment shots. Almost like candids. Can be at any time, day or night." After last night, I had a feeling the night shoots weren't nearly as innocent as I'd been led to believe. Not that I was too worried. I would make sure I wasn't alone with Jean-Claude, and all would be well.

"I don't like this," Ryland said.

"Me neither," I said, not exactly referring to the ghost alone. "But I do want the cover. It's my chance to break into the world of fashion modeling. Therefore, I'm going to try and ignore the warning bells in my head."

"But—" he began.

"We'll have to discuss it later. I'm late as it is." Without another word, I headed outside to the pool, where the other models huddled around in various stages of undress, vaping fruity mixtures. The sun eased the rest of my tension.

For now, I had to focus on the job, on doing what I was hired to do.

The poor models around me, who wore some form of black leather in the seventy-degree heat, looked as if they had witnessed a far greater evil than the ghost. Sweat dripped from their tanned skin as the sun burned down.

The pool glimmered, looking fresh and inviting, much more so than the models who now openly sneered at me.

I liked people and wanted them to like me in return. From the looks of the clammy models, however, liking me was far down on their to-do lists. Except with Stephi. She raised her hand to wave, but one look at the apparent leader of the group, June, and her arm dropped.

Holding his head as if it pained him, Jean-Claude glared at the group of models, and then turned back to me. "Are you ready?" he asked in a hoarse whisper.

I nodded, excitement building. This was my chance.

"Great," he said, in a tone that suggested it was anything but. Obviously Jean-Claude was suffering from last night's debauchery. "We'll start with some shots of you, posing like

Marilyn on the diving board, staring into the water. Do you think you can do that?"

"Of course."

"Good." His head wobbled, and then he winced. "Now the rest of you"—he motioned to the melting models in leather as if punishing each one for some unknown slight—"I want you on your knees, crawling along the edges as if waiting to attack."

The girls reluctantly took their places around the poolside. The concrete must've been at least a hundred degrees on their bare skin. I suddenly felt sorry for them.

Then two of them made mooing sounds at me. My empathy withered in an instant.

Head high, I took to the stage.

Or in this case, a long, tad-slippery diving board.

That was when the first explosion occurred.

CHAPTER 6

THANKFULLY, THE EXPLOSIONS were nothing more than the bright flashbulbs misfiring, which caused the glass tubes to burst. Be that as it may, I nearly peed myself when the first exploded, thinking the electrical ghost from last night was after me.

"Let's take five while we get another flash set up." Jean-Claude smiled until he was facing his assistants; then his expression darkened. "What the hell, Roger? Ethan? I told you to be careful when you set up those flare flashes."

"We were," Roger—or was it Ethan?—declared in a near whine.

Not wanting to disturb the budding argument, I slipped off the diving board. The other models stood in a protective group poolside, giving me their backs. I debated jumping in to join them. I was sure that after they got to know me, they'd stop hating me. I understood their resentment. I was new to the business, and yet I was going to be on the cover. Had the situation been reversed, I wasn't sure how welcoming I'd be either. Then again, I doubted I'd be downright rude. It just wasn't in me.

Before I decided whether to join the models, coldness swept over me, even under the bright sun. I shivered, reaching for a towel to wrap around my shoulders. Exhaling, my breath came out in an icy fog. I glanced at the circle of other women. They looked fine. Not one goose bump between them.

The barest of touches, like the hands of death itself, brushed my back.

The blond hairs on my neck rose to attention. I yelped as, from behind me, something gave me a shove, propelling me forward.

Unfortunately, I ran directly into the path of Ethan.

Or maybe it was Roger.

Either way, I watched in horror as he started to pinwheel toward the pool, expensive photography equipment in tow. I managed to grab his Gucci belt, barely steadying us both. Luckily, all of the equipment remained intact.

Once he settled back in place, I spun to see who had pushed me. But no one was there.

A nervous giggle formed on my lips.

"What is wrong with you?" the assistant asked, in a tone that suggested he couldn't care less. Without waiting for an explanation, he huffed off.

What was going on? I swear someone or something had pushed me.

Was it *possible* . . .

No way. I must've tripped or something, I reassured myself, smoothing down my white dress. No matter how many times I repeated it, however, I didn't believe it.

I could almost feel the cold fingertips pressed against my flesh.

A scream, much like the one I heard last night, shook me from my thoughts.

Unlike last night, instead of a ghost, I looked up in time to see the models dodging bird droppings from a flock of pigeons flying overhead. If I'd still been standing where I was prior to the invisible shove, the turd bombing would've struck me dead-on.

I guess I owed the ghost one.

The models ran off to their hotel rooms to wash off.

"Okay, Loey," Jean-Claude called a few minutes later. "I think we're ready for you again."

"But the other . . ." I waved to the missing models.

"We'll just do the close-ups on you until they get back."

I nodded, moving to the diving board once again. I placed the towel I'd had around my neck for warmth on a deck chair. The sun was back in play, and the sky looked clear of birds threatening to bomb my outfit.

Carefully, I climbed the ladder to the diving board, the grit of which tickled my bare toes as the wood wobbled under me. I held out my arms to steady myself. Last thing I needed was a cooling dip into the chlorine waters. Green hair would not go well with this outfit.

"Now, Loey," Jean-Claude said. "Look this way." He pointed to the right. I slowly turned my face until he told me to stop. "Now, give me a smirk."

Easy enough. I did as he asked, mimicking an expression on his face. The camera whirled as the newly affixed flash popped. The light burned my eyes for a second. I blinked until the glowing circles left my eyes.

"Beautiful. Now take a step forward," he said, motioning me ahead.

I took a timid step to the edge of the board. It sunk down, nearly upending me into the water below. Thankfully I stayed on top and dry.

"Perfect," Jean-Claude said, the camera whirling again. "Stay exactly like that."

Easy for him to say.

Especially when loud cracking sounded from the wooden board.

I glanced down in time to watch the board split in two. My arms flailed, but I still didn't have the ability to fly, much to my dismay, as I hit the cold, deep water below.

Water swallowed me, sucking me toward the bottom of the pool. Luckily, I'd managed to suck in a full breath before I hit the water. Once I finished my descent, I started to push off the swirled tiles of the pool to the bright, sunny day above.

But something or someone held fast.

My body failed to comply with my brain's order to kick free. Instead my feet felt like lead, weighing me down. Soon my body became drowsy, as if drugged. My mind floated on a cloud of pink. I was drowning. Even as my mind worked that out, I could do nothing to save myself.

Just as quickly as it had started, the drugged feeling vanished.

I kicked against the pool tiles, shooting through the water to the wondrousness of the oxygen above.

CHAPTER 7

TWO HOURS LATER, I was back in the safe confines of the bungalow, finally dry and dressed in a pair of my favorite jeggings and an oversize tee. I finger-combed my freshly dried hair as I recounted my dive into the depths of modeling for my friends as well as for my online LitSquad in the form of a vlog.

"Hey, my loves," I said into the camera. "Today has been a weird one. My first day on the shoot for *FAS* and I managed to fall into the pool as well as into the supernatural. Seriously. I think a ghost tried to kill me after I splashed into the pool.

It was so bizarre. One minute, I'm fine. And then I couldn't move. It was like I was drugged."

I paused, remembering those terrifying moments when my brain accepted my fate.

"And then the drugged feeling vanished, and I shot from the water."

V, Chase, and Ryland gasped. For the first time, V looked unsure, but quickly covered it. She would never believe in ghosts, not until she became one. Chase looked intrigued by my story, while Ryland's face had paled.

"While the chlorine won't do wonders for my hair, the worst part of the day—aside from nearly dying, that is—was when I emerged from the water, gulping mouthfuls of clean-ish air, and"—I licked my lips—"on the side of the pool stood the very wet, highly acclaimed photographer Jean-Claude Petit, with a very expensive camera in his hands and a grimace on his face. Apparently my unintentional belly flop had created quite a wave, splashing over the edge of the pool, soaking everyone within five feet. Jean-Claude quickly canceled the rest of the day's shoot."

My friends took turns offering their condolences.

"I suspect this might be my first and last cover shoot," I said to the camera.

On that note, I ended the vlog with a promise to update my subscribers on tomorrow's shoot as well as any ghostly contact.

"Oh, bae," Chase said. "You need to do something fun to take your mind off of today."

"Yeah," V agreed. "What is on your Cali bucket list?"

I smiled at my friends. "Well, I did hope to see the Hammer Museum before I left."

"Then it's your lucky day," Chase said.

A little art therapy was just what I needed to distract myself from my near-death experience. The Hammer Museum was a perfect choice, as it housed one of the largest collections of California artists.

As well as not a hint of the supernatural.

I wouldn't go as far as saying what happened in the pool had anything to do with what I saw last night or in the mirror this morning.

I didn't have to.

Not when Chase said as much for me.

"This is crazy," he said. "It has to be the ghost. The only other explanation is a series of unexplained, random events."

V wrapped her arms over her chest. "Not the only other explanation."

"What do you mean?" I asked, tilting my head, which caused the water stuck inside my inner ear to slosh to the side. "What else could it be?"

"We all know YouTubers who take things too far to gain subscribers." She bit her lip. "People who might stage something like this."

The Ghost-Hunting Twin Brothers Grimm came instantly to mind. They had a well-watched channel that offered an assortment of supposed ghost hunts. Not that I paid it much attention. Or at least not to the ghost hunting part. Instead, I spent time staring at the beauty of one Damien Grimm.

If only he wasn't such a jerk.

Chase brought me back to the discussion at hand. "No way," he said. "This isn't a trick. This ghost is very real, according to my sources, and after Loey. We have to stop it."

Terror tickled the back of my throat. The pain of it aside, death would suck for plenty of reasons. One being the fact I hadn't finished watching *The Vampire Diaries*. Plus, my furbabies, Maka and Annie, would miss me terribly. "It did feel like someone or something held me down in the water." I hugged my knees to my chest.

"Let's bust this ghost bitch," Chase said.

"Don't listen to him," Ryland said, waving to our friend. "V is right. Someone is punking you."

V placed her hands on her hips and let out a sigh. "And if we leave, they win." With a frown she added, "And that doesn't sit well. Not at all."

My back straightened, as did my resolve. "You're right. Whatever this is, I'm not going to let it ruin my modeling dreams."

V laughed. "Not quite what I meant, but attagirl!"

"Let's strategize while we get some art therapy on!" I pointed to the front door of the bungalow, charging my troop of best friends forth. With the excitement of the excursion ahead of us, I led our squad into the midday sun.

And smack into the unimaginable.

Literally.

CHAPTER 8

"WELL, WELL, IF it isn't Loey's little LitSquad," Dante Grimm said, rubbing the whiskers on his chin. "I thought I smelled overprivileged and overrated prima donnas."

I sneered back at him as anger rushed through my veins. "Amazing you can smell anything, considering the sense of smell takes a thousand brain cells. I doubt you have that many." I glanced from him to his identical twin, Damien. "Even between you."

Damien, who'd remained silent so far, lips twitched.

I went on. "I was going to ask what the Twin Brothers Grimm are doing here, but I'm sure I already know the answer."

"And what's that?" Damien finally spoke, asking in a slow drawl as though we had all the time in the world.

I flashed back to our first meeting, and that same damn drawl.

A year or so ago, I'd stopped off at a famous bakery in my hometown for a birthday cake for my brother. While there, I'd run into Damien. Literally. Smack dab into his chest.

In typical Loey fashion, the cake in my arms flipped upward, covering me in frosting.

Just then I noticed the video camera in his twin brother Dante's hand. Dante had caught the embarrassing incident on camera. Damien swore, his voice husky and sweet, they wouldn't use the footage on their channel.

I trusted him to keep his word. Trusted his honey-soaked words. Trusted his emerald gaze. Trusted him when he asked me to grab a coffee with him once I cleaned up. Dressed in a cute, clean jumpsuit, I'd waited at the coffee shop for over an hour.

He never showed.

Two days later, a cruel snapshot from the video appeared on Instagram with the caption, "Fat Girl in a Bikini Eats Entire Cake." I wasn't wearing a bikini at the time, but lies ran rampant on the web. Shame had burned my cheeks when I first saw the image.

In that moment, I grew to hate the Grimm twins—Damien especially, for his betrayal.

Chase pushed in front of me, bringing me back to the present. He glared into the scruffy face of the second twin, Dante. "Loey's right," he said. "Unexplainable 'paranormal' things happen, the shoot is halted, and suddenly you two idiots show up." He sighed as he glanced back at me. "I didn't want to believe it, but this has to be fake."

"Told you," V muttered under her breath. "No such thing as ghosts."

Dante's eyes narrowed. "What are you talking about?"

Chase rolled his eyes as he turned back to Dante. "Don't play dumb. The haunting you're currently faking here to boost your subscriber count. But guess what? It's not going to work." He shook his head. "People on the Internet are too smart to fall for this fake ghost crap."

Hadn't I just fallen for this fake ghost crap? I stifled a smile. Chase, while passionate, was entirely wrong. Too often people fell for fake news stories, facts, and profiles. Clickbaiting and catfishing were all too common in this industry.

Along with weirdos asking to buy your urine for fifty dollars a pop.

But that was a tale for another time.

The Twin Brothers Grimm weren't on the buying urine level of creepy. Yet. I vowed that if I learned they were the ones messing with me, I would get payback. "Fake ghost crap?" Damien's gaze narrowed on mine, over the top of Chase's head. For not only did the brothers have more subscribers than Chase; they both stood at least four inches above his five-foot, eight-inch frame. "Tell me what happened," Damien ordered.

"Why, so you can exploit Loey again? Forget it." Chase grabbed my arm, rushing forward. I dug my heels in, unable to look away from the concern on Damien's much-too-handsome face.

He called to me softly, "Loey . . ."

"Not that I'm buying your innocent act, but—" I began.

Chase held up his hand. "Loey. Don't."

"It's okay," I said, to reassure him. I turned back to face Damien. "Last night and then again this morning, I . . . think . . . I saw a ghost."

Dante looked excited by the prospect, but his twin was less pleased. "Where? What did she look like?" Damien's face tightened. "Did she speak to you?"

I shook my head, and he seemed to relax.

"Why?" I asked. "What does her talking have anything to do with—"

"Doesn't matter," he said. "I want you to check out of this hotel right now. Pack up your bags and go somewhere else. There's a great place on Sunset Boulevard, ghost-free, and with way better views than this hotel."

V laughed at this. "You boys must really be scared that Loey's going to figure out your little 'ghost' tricks and tell the world. And you're right. Be afraid. Be very afraid. There is no way you're gonna convince us that this place is haunted." V moved in front of me, breaking the stare-off Damien and I currently found ourselves in. "We're going to prove it's a hoax. Right, LitSquad?"

As a battle cry, it wasn't the greatest, but we still rallied around it.

Damien just shook his head slowly, while his twin looked downright angry at the statement. V took my hand and pulled me around the brothers. I tried not to inhale Damien's manly musk as we passed. Mostly because manly musk cologne had proved to be my downfall a time or four.

Getting mixed up with a man like him would be a bad, bad idea.

Even if he did look great in a pair of Levi's.

"Can you believe those guys? What losers," Chase said a few hours later, as we finished the tour of the Hammer Museum. While sometimes I didn't understand it, contemporary pop art appealed to me in unexplainable ways, much like the supernatural itself.

Even though Chase was still annoyed by the arrival of the ghost-hunting twins, I wished he'd let it go and instead enjoy the beauty of the sculpture gardens we currently found ourselves in. Stones jutted into the sky, cold to the touch and so beautiful it stole your breath. "Everyone knows they fake it," he said. "So now they're suddenly real ghost hunters? What a joke."

I tilted my head, surprised by his anger. Apparently he knew the twins' channel better than I did. From what I'd seen, they did exactly what they were doing now: arriving at the scene of a haunting to put an end to the ghostly antics. Supposedly freeing the spirits of the undead so they could find some peace. And looking hot while doing it.

Which was what brought Damien to the Kansas bakery a year ago. And to our ill-fated meeting. The memory of our meeting burned forever in my memory.

"You look good enough to eat," he joked as cake fell in clumps from my hair after I'd run into his hard chest, knocking cake and frosting into my face.

I glowered up at him. "Don't say another word."

Instead of speaking, he ran his thumb down the side of my cheek. White frosting covered the digit. He licked it off in such an exaggerated way, I couldn't help but laugh. "How about I buy you a coffee to make up for my standing still while you smashed into me?" he said with a grin.

I heaved a loud sigh. "I suppose."

"Meet you at the diner up the street?"

I nodded.

"This hunt shouldn't take more than an hour." His eyes flickered over my frosting-stained hair. "Is that enough time?" He held up

a helpless hand. "I'll wait all night for you, Loey Lane. Maybe my whole life."

How could I stupidly have fallen for his charm? He hadn't meant a word of it. The proof was in his standing me up and, later, embarrassing me with the Instagram pic.

Damien Grimm was not to be trusted.

No matter how sincere his concern sounded when we'd run into him and his dim-witted twin earlier.

The LitSquad, and my subscribers following along at home, believed, like V did, that the haunting at the hotel was fake. No matter how real it might feel. I pulled out my iPhone, checking the latest tweets under *#Next2Die* currently trending. I wasn't sure who had started the hashtag, but it seemed to stick, as did the belief the Grimm twins were fakers.

Albeit gorgeous ones. I tweeted my LitSquad with a new question.

> @Loeybug: Am I #Next2Die like
> @GrimmTwins want us to believe?
> @BeMore: Don't trust those boys
> @JJWilliams: No such things as ghosts
> @realTrustME: That one twin is HOT AF

"Those twins need to be exposed," Chase said, echoing the online sentiment.

I barely heard him. I was too busy staring at the candid of Damien someone had tweeted my way. Even under poorly drawn devil horns, he was flawless. Did his skin feel as warm as it looked? A new tweet popped up.

@GrimmTwins: Not going to let that happen
@Loeybug. U can trust me.

My stomach fluttered as I read Damien's tweet. I ignored the sensation like I did his tweet. As much as my heart urged me to buy into his sincerity. But that would only lead to me sitting alone in a diner waiting for Damien like a fool. I wouldn't fall under his spell again.

"Right, Loey?" Chase's voice echoed.

I blinked my way back into reality and looked at my friends. "W-What? Sorry, I kinda zoned out."

"Just say yes," V said. "If only to shut him up."

I hesitated, finally agreeing to who knows what. "Yes."

"Good." Chase smirked, showing off perfectly white, capped teeth purchased with daddy's credit card. "Tonight it is on. Operation Twins Suck is a go."

I frowned. Just what had I agreed to?

My worries faded as something drew my eyes to the grassy field across the way. Right smack in skyscrapers and smog. "What's over there?" I asked the hometown boy, Chase.

He followed my gaze. "Westwood Village."

"What's that?" V asked, her arm around Ryland.

"You don't know?"

The three of us shook our collective heads.

"That's were Marilyn's buried."

"Really?" My stomach fluttered. "Can we go inside, see her grave?"

Ryland flashed me a quick grin. "Are you sure, Loey? It's getting dark. We don't want to be stuck in the graveyard at night."

V smacked his arm. "Don't be a jerk."

As much as I wanted to explain, I couldn't. The words just wouldn't come. But I needed to see her grave. Needed to feel the energy around it. It was almost elemental. "Please" was all I could say.

As if he knew the feeling, Chase took my arm, leading us to the buried, literally, secret graveyard of Hollywood.

CHAPTER 9

THREE MINUTES LATER, we found ourselves at the West-wood Village Memorial Park Cemetery, which sat on a single square city block, nestled among skyscrapers and other assorted buildings. Even with the drought, the green of the cemetery lawns sparkled with life, at odds wit the famous inhabitants buried beneath.

Row after row of burial plaques crossed the landscape, almost all of them belonged to Hollywood elite from bygone days. Frank Zappa called this place his final resting home. I smiled, thinking of my dad's collection of band tees. He'd loved Frank Zappa.

Chase walked us to the north side of the white stone crypt that shelved the dead. Marilyn Monroe's tomb sat proudly in the second row, backlit with the glow of the setting California sun. A peace unlike any I'd ever experienced settled around me. On the front of the crypt was a small bronze plaque with *Marilyn Monroe* scrawled across it. The dates *1926–1962* sat underneath the letters. A pink color stained the front of the tomb where she lay in what I hoped was eternal rest.

Before I asked, Chase said, "It's lipstick."

"What?" I asked, leaning for a closer look. I rubbed my finger against the color. Sure enough, Chase was right. Lipstick stained the wall. The same crimson color I'd seen in the swirling ghost mist. I tried to banish the thought, but it remained, nagging at me.

"So many people have kissed the wall in her honor, the marker became stained." Chase handed me a tissue from his pocket. It was rumpled but otherwise unused. I wiped my finger. Tears unexpectedly grew in my eyes. Like me, Marilyn had struggled with depression and anxiety. And in the end, it took her life, at the young age of thirty-six.

I vowed to do her justice on the *FAS* cover.

I stared at the grave for quite some time. Eventually my LitSquad ventured off to explore the other famous gravestones. Graves of people who had died decades before we were born, like Janet Leigh, star of the infamous shower scene in *Psycho*.

In the golden age of Hollywood, movies sure were different, as were the stars. Had wide-eyed Norma Jeane Mortenson looked up at this very sky like I was doing now? Had she felt the same chill in the air of the approaching dusk? Had the whispers of possibility filled her with the very excitement brewing in my belly?

For some time, I stood there, looking at the sky, as I kept silent vigil at Marilyn's side.

As it finally sank below the horizon, the sun bathed the graveyard in a soft pink light. The glow of which, like the lipstick stain, reminded me of the pink ghost mist. Shivers ran through my body. I rubbed my arms, and that's when I noticed him.

Or her.

Or whatever gender the person in the creepy clown mask identified as, for from my vantage point about a hundred feet away, I wasn't quite sure. The clown was slim and not overly tall, wearing black pants and a festive joker top. A rubber mask covered its face. While I'd seen my fair share of creepy clowns lurking around, especially after the recent mass hysteria and sightings, this one was different.

For one thing, the clown just stood there, in the middle of the graveyard.

Staring at me. Right at me.

I looked to the right and then to the left.

No one else was around.

Where had the LitSquad gone? I swallowed a wave of anxiety. I refused to play into the creepy clown phenomena. Rather than run from the clown, I dug my heels in, and stared it down. Upon reflection, I must've appeared somewhat insane.

But I wasn't going to back down. I'd been pushed around enough for one day, first by the spirit in the mirror and then by some invisible force at the pool.

"Loey?" V said as she came around the corner of the tomb. "What's wrong?"

I turned toward her, pointing to the clown.

"What? Did you see another 'ghost'?" she asked with mistrust.

I glanced back to the spot where the clown had stood only moments before. "You . . . didn't see . . . a clown over there a second ago?"

"A clown? No. Was one of those creepy clown pranksters hanging around?" She rushed forward, yelling at the empty space. "It's not funny, you idiots. Someone is going to get killed."

I grabbed her arm before she could go any further. "Forget it. It's gone." Even as I said those words, the hairs on my neck rose. Something was off about that clown.

"Hey, ladies." Chase appeared at our side. "What say you about some dinner? And then I have a surprise in store for you this evening."

My gaze went back to the empty space, and then to Chase. "Please tell me it doesn't involve ghosts or clowns," I said. "I really can't take much more."

CHAPTER 10

I SHOULD'VE ADDED mean models to that list.

Unfortunately, by the time I realized it, it was far too late.

Chase's surprise was beyond the expected. Not only had he gotten us bottle service in the VIP section of Lure, a club about a ten minutes' drive from the hotel, for a meet and greet, but he'd invited everyone from the photo shoot. I wasn't sure how he'd arranged it on such short notice, and after a drink or two, I really didn't care.

Occasionally I did meet and greets. It was the perfect arrangement for meeting my LitSquad members in person. Often I had them at places like Taco Bell, Starbucks, or a retail mall. I'd never had one at a nightclub. But I agreed to go since Chase looked so excited by the idea.

When we pulled to the curb outside the nightclub, men and women stood behind velvet ropes, waiting for the bouncer to give them the nod. Much to my surprise, Chase exited the limo and the bouncer unlocked the velvet ropes to let us in without pause or fuss. A new experience for me, as I'd spent many hours waiting in line at clubs. Not that Kansas offered much in the way of nightlife, unless one wore a cowboy hat and pointed boots.

A cute hostess in a sleek black dress led us to a cozy spot next to the stage. I suspected the cost of the VIP section was more than I made in a month. Chase slipped the hostess his black Amex card. "Two bottles of Elit magnum and a couple of the Ace of Spades," he said as if he wasn't ordering ten thousand dollars' worth of alcohol. "Get them whatever they want"—he motioned to the LitSquad—"and keep the tab open."

It must be nice to have enough money to buy whatever you want without a second thought. My liberal guilt grew as I sipped the bubbly champagne a few minutes later. "Relax, Loey," Chase said. "If it will make you feel better, I'll donate whatever we spend tonight to the animal rescue. Okay?"

I nodded. I knew a part of Chase resented the wealth, the hypocrisy of it all. Resented his absentee father. Maybe spending frivolously was his way of paying his father back. I also knew he'd do just what he said. Chase, for all his frat-boy mannerisms, was a man of his word.

The music swelled around us with pulsing beats. The DJ, only a few feet away, bobbed his head in time. Sweat-slicked bodies moved to the music, often intertwined so you couldn't tell where one started and the other stopped. My body grew light, my head swimming from the alcohol. I didn't drink all that often, so when I did, it hit me quickly and hard.

June, the model who'd sent Jean-Claude tumbling into the pool, suddenly appeared at our table. She looked beautiful in a maroon sheath dress, as expected, though dark lines circled her eyes. She took the drink Chase offered, not bothering to thank him.

"Bummer about the shoot getting canceled today," I yelled over the swell of music.

She finally glanced my way, frowning slightly. "Do I know you?"

Before I even answered, she drained her glass, handed it to me like I was her personal waitstaff, and promptly lost interest in me. I swallowed a sharp retort.

Chase ordered another round, though we had barely dented the first. Once the waitress brought the bottles, he signed yet another black Amex card receipt with flourish. The card gleamed as the flashing red stage lights hit it just right.

June's face flickered with emotion.

As if narrowing in on wealthy prey, she put her arm on Chase's, pulling him toward the dance floor lit with bright white lights. The dancers seemed to glow, like flickering candles. "Let's dance," she said.

He looked at me. I gave him a small smile. June led him off as Stephi, the model far too young to be at the club, let alone drunk at the club, approached. She swayed slightly on her four-inch heels. A man old enough to be her grandfather caught her around the waist, and held on.

A sick feeling rose in my stomach. "Stephi," I said. "Come sit with me." I patted the comfortable red leather sofa. She drunkenly dropped down, and the older guy shot me a glare. I grinned back. When an ice cube flew out of her glass, hitting Ryland, who sat a seat away, in the head, I took her drink.

"You have pretty hair," she said, running her fingers through my blond mane.

"Thanks."

She leaned against me. "I'm drunk."

"I can see that."

"I'm happy you're here instead of Emily," she muttered. "She's such a snob. Just because she has a rich boyfriend."

I frowned. "I thought she was with Jean-Claude."

"That's what he thought too." Giggles ensued. "But she was in love with someone else."

"Is that so?" Not that I wanted to gossip, but I was worried something bad had happened to Emily. If she merely ran off with a rich boyfriend, I'd feel much better. Though she had left her makeup case. . . .

"It made June so mad."

"Why?"

She shook her head. "She was in love with Jean-Claude. But when she found out he was sleeping with Emily too, she exploded."

I couldn't really blame her. I would've done much the same. "What did she do?"

"She told him Emily had a boyfriend," she said, in what she might've thought was a whisper, but the sound carried halfway across the club even with the pulsing music. "And that he was a fool. Emily didn't care about Jean-Claude at all. She was just using him. That he was her *photographer with benefits*, and that was it."

Ouch, that had to hurt.

"He begged June to take him back. But she wouldn't." Drunken laughter bubbled from Stephi's throat. "He blamed Emily for it."

"What do you mean?" I asked. Had Jean-Claude hurt her? My stomach tingled with fear.

"You're pretty," she said. Her head fell against the back of the sofa, rolling to the side.

"Stephi?" I said.

Her eyelids fluttered open, and then closed as she passed out again.

Chase returned to the table, none too steady on his feet, June suspiciously absent. When I asked about it, he said, "She's not my type. Too brittle."

"Do me a favor," I said to him. "Keep watch over Stephi for a second."

He shot me a sloppy grin. "Anything for you, Loey-bug." With that, he plopped down on the couch next to her, the drink in his hand sloshing on his pants. He laughed, holding up his empty glass so the waitress could see he needed another round.

When she came to take his order, I shook off the next round, and instead headed for the restroom. It was jam-packed with girls arranging and rearranging cleavage and reapplying lipstick. I scooted my way to a long mirror covered in lipstick kisses. Not one of which was the same color stained on Marilyn's grave, for which I was grateful. I needed some time away from the dead.

I checked my makeup, opting for a refresher while I waited for a stall to open. I pulled out my eyebrow pencil, my hand trembling only slightly.

"Is it really you?" a girl in tight leather pants and a tank top screamed over the music. I glanced around. Was she talking to me? *Apparently so,* I thought, when she threw her arms around my waist and lifted me from my feet.

"Hi—" I began.

She cut me off, squeezing me tighter. "You're why I'm here. I've wanted to meet you for, like, ever. When I saw you'd be here . . . I just love you!"

"Ow, my heart," I said, tears burning my eyes. "I love you too." Meeting my LitSquad always brightened my mood. And this girl more than most after the crappy day I'd had.

The girl released me. "I used to get teased about my weight."

My eyebrow rose. The poor thing was far from obese. Maybe ten or fifteen pounds overweight, but it looked great on her. What was wrong with people? You don't build yourself up when you tear others down, no matter how it might feel like it in the moment. "Some people are beyond stupid."

She nodded. "I stumbled across your *Fat Girl in a Bikini* series, and it changed my life. You stand there, beautiful, with confidence. I wanted to be like that."

I gave her a small smile. "You *are* like that."

"Thank you." Her eyes burned into mine. "For everything."

With renewed passion for body confidence in my heart, I started back to the table, but a hand on my arm stopped me. I spun to the person holding me, ready to unleash.

The words died on my lips.

"What are you doing here?" Damien Grimm, in all his good-looking glory, towered over me. His fingers burned against my already-heated skin.

I raised an eyebrow at his heavy-handed tone. "I don't see how that's your business."

"Loey," he growled in warning. "Will you just let it go? I had nothing to do with that photo of you wearing that cake. Though I'll admit I have it as my screen saver." He flashed his phone in my direction. Sure enough, my image, smeared in cake, appeared on-screen.

Rage burned inside me at his mocking, not to mention his lack of apology for standing me up a year ago. Honestly, that had hurt more than the birthday cake photo. In high school, I struggled with romantic entanglements. Too often I'd given my heart without an authentic return. So when Damien had stood me up, those high school insecurities surfaced once again. "Even if I believed you, which I don't, it doesn't matter," I said. "There is nothing between us. Nor will there ever be."

He stepped closer, pulling my body toward him. "Are you sure?" His mouth hovered inches from mine. "Because I think there just might be."

I pulled back, yanking his hand from my arm. "Completely," I said, feeling anything but. Something dangerous sparked between us. He was like chocolate chip cookie dough, dangerous and irresistible at the same time. Good thing I'd lost my sweet tooth years ago. Mostly. Now I settled for savory treats.

"Now, if you'll excuse me ..." I didn't wait for his response—not that I could've heard it over the music—and walked away, my head high.

While my demeanor appeared confident inside, I was shaking. The power Damien wielded was more than my body could withstand. Better to keep far, far away from him.

I headed to the table, slightly breathless.

V, sweat dripping from her brow from dancing, tilted her head. "What's up? You look like you've seen a ghost," she joked.

I shot her an eye roll. I glanced around to where I'd left Chase and Stephi. "Where are Chase and Stephi?"

Ryland pointed to the corner, where Chase was passed out next to the young model. Both lay slumped over on the couch. I looked closer to make sure both of them were still breathing. Thankfully the answer was yes. "Shall we wake them up?"

"Naw," V said with a shake of her head. Wetness flew from the ends of her hair. "We'll tip the bartenders an extra hundred to pour them into the limo and get them back to the hotel."

"Are you sure they'll be all right?" I chewed on my bottom lip.

V grinned. "Tonight, yes. Tomorrow morning, I doubt it." She paused, rubbing her stomach. "I'm starving. Let's go get some munchies."

Ryland, not one to turn down munchies of any kind, nodded in agreement. He was our designated sober friend tonight, a must-have for young women at clubs. Too many bad things could happen if you didn't have someone to watch your back, and your drink.

I thought of the man clinging to Stephi and shivered.

Linking arms with me and V, Ryland worked our way through the throng and out the club door. Before we exited, I glanced back, searching the crowd. I was a big enough woman to admit, I wanted one last look at the man I vowed to avoid at all costs.

I caught sight of Damien across the room.

He too was leaving.

But unlike me, he wasn't leaving alone. A tall, model-thin woman with dark hair pulled him out the door. I didn't see her face, but the rest of the image was sheared into my mind.

"Loey?" V asked quietly. "You okay?"

"Peachy," I said, swinging my attention back to the fresh air beyond the club door and the love of my LitSquad.

They were all I genuinely needed.

Along with my furbabies, of course.

The night sounds swelled around us. Cars roared along the well-lit streets at reckless speeds. A diner sign flashed in neon pink across the street.

We managed to jaywalk across the road without incident. Once we entered the diner, a young, blue-haired waitress sat us, pouring coffee without questions. A few minutes later fluffy pancakes appeared as well.

The perfect ending to a pretty crappy day.

I pledged tomorrow would be better.

Unless the woman in the mirror, her creepy clown compatriot, and Damien Grimm had other ideas.

CHAPTER 11

AN HOUR LATER, I stalked through the hotel lobby. Quicker than normal, given the amount of coffee I had running through my veins from our after-club indulgence. Ryland held my arm in one hand and V's in the other. I shoved a hand into my bag, searching for that key card. When I finally located it, I held it in the air like a prize. "I got it."

He shushed me. "It's two in the morning. Keep it down before you get us thrown out."

I nodded solemnly, which turned into a giggle. I tried to stifle it. But more laughs slipped through my lips. I was still a little intoxicated, but thankfully, my head had stopped swimming.

Ryland rolled his eyes, reaching for my arm again. V moved in before his arm made contact. She leaned against him, running her hand up his chest. Ryland swallowed hard. I turned away before V made her move. Poor Ryland never stood a chance.

He'd been in love with V for years. And she occasionally used his adoration, and him, when convenient or when thoroughly inebriated, which seemed like the case tonight.

Putting one hand over my ear to muffle Ryland's groan, I slid the key card into the lock from the hotel to the pool, where my bungalow sat with its inviting, large bed. All I wanted to do now was slip into the silky sheets and forget the scary events of the day.

As I walked to my room, I paused to glance up at the moon, its light shining brightly in the LA sky. I could see the outline of the Hollywood sign, the sign supposedly haunted by starlet Peg Entwistle, who jumped to her death from it in 1932.

So many ghost stories here.

While I missed my home, I also loved this city. Loved the vibrations and night songs.

I pulled out my iPhone, preparing to capture the sight of the Hollywood sign for my virtual LitSquad. A loud splash jerked me from my musings. Water drenched my dress. Half in shock, I looked down at it, and then to the pool.

I blinked.

And still I couldn't comprehend what I saw in front of me.

I wiped at my eyes, dropping my handbag in the process.

When my brain began to function again, allowing my vocal cords full command, I let out an earsplitting scream. Dogs all over California barked. Windows shook. People grabbed for their earthquake kits. Lights exploded all over the pool area as my screams woke hotel guests.

Ryland came running, his breathing labored. V followed behind in a stumble-run. "What the hell, Loey?" Ryland yelled, jerking me from my terrified screams.

I pointed at the pool. To the same place I'd seen the spirit the night before. My tongue failed to form words, or at least comprehensible ones.

Ryland looked where I pointed, and a scream ripped from his throat too. He was quicker to return to sanity. "Call nine-one-one," he yelled as he ran for the pool, diving into the water like a knife through butter. Fat-free butter. So, really, sort of jerky, with plenty of splashing and unhappiness.

I glanced down at the phone that, for some reason, I was already holding. Right. I was mid-vlog when the splash occurred. I closed down the video app, dialed the numbers, surprisingly in the right order, and waited. And waited. This was LA, at two in the morning. One of their busier times.

Finally, a tired voice answered. "Nine-one-one, what's your emergency?"

"I . . . ah . . . think someone's dead. In the pool."

The worn-out voice perked up, and in the background I overheard the voice say, "Hey, Bob. We got another one." A few seconds later, the voice returned to the line. "Are you sure they're dead?"

I glanced at the bloody pool, then to the top of the hotel where the person must've jumped from. "Pretty sure."

A sigh. "Cops will be there in an hour. Stay where you are, and for the love of God, don't touch anything."

"Right." I winced as Ryland pulled the body from the depths of the water. "When you say *anything*, you mean . . ."

"Not a thing."

"Gotcha," I said, hanging up. My stomach rolled, and a trail of half-digested pancakes erupted from my lips, spilling into the already-contaminated pool.

CHAPTER 12

"MISS, IS THIS your vomit?" a pale-faced man in a horrible, ill-fitting blue uniform with "LAPD" on the back asked as he scooped and bagged my puke. I turned away, afraid I'd toss my cookies again. "Miss?" he insisted.

I blew out a harsh, thankfully minty (after a half pack of mints) breath. "Yes."

"Don't fret." His lips curved into a kind smile. "Happens all the time. If I had a dime for every time a bystander yakked on a crime scene. Sometimes even on the deceased—"

"Jerry!" a woman dressed in a black pantsuit yelled at the talkative tech. "Enough. Bring me the report, and get back to the body." He ran off to do her bidding as the woman headed my way. "You there. Did you make the call to nine-one-one?"

I nodded.

She gave me a tight smile. "I'm young."

I nodded, not wanting to hurt her feelings. The crow's-feet lining her eyes and the laugh lines etching her lips suggested she was closer to middle age. "Okay, if you say so."

She started a half eye roll, then must've thought better of it. "My name is Detective *Young*." She pulled out a small leather notebook and a pen. "Can you tell me exactly what you saw?"

"I didn't see anything. Not really."

Her eyebrow rose.

"I mean . . . I saw the body . . . but only after . . ." I pointed to the sky.

"Right." She licked the tip of the pen, a disgusting habit, and then started to write. "Before the victim landed in the pool, did you hear anything? Like a scream? Or a fight?"

I thought back, replaying the events. "No. I don't remember hearing anything." I bit my lip. "That's odd, right? Not hearing a scream?"

She lifted her shoulders into a noncommittal shrug.

"If the . . . victim fell or even if they jumped . . . they would've screamed, right?" I sure as hell would've made some noise. Kicking and screaming was how I planned to go out. None of that quiet-into-the-night stuff for me.

Her shoulders raised again. "Did you recognize the victim?"

"Of course not. I barely saw him."

"Her," she corrected, suspicion lacing her words.

My eyes narrowed. What was going on? Why was she acting like I was a killer? "Her," I repeated.

"And yet you're staying in the very bungalow where the victim is registered."

"What!?" My stomach rolled again. It couldn't be Emily Cook. It couldn't be.

But Young confirmed my worst fears. "The victim's name is Emily Cook." Young watched my face like a vulture searches for prey. "Did you know her?"

I swallowed down a rush of bile rising from my stomach. "Not really."

"Then what are you doing in the room registered to her?"

I shrugged as tears burned my eyes. "The hotel was booked solid."

"Is that right?" She nodded to a man I hadn't noticed before, probably because of his brown suit and average height and features. Plus, the limited amount of brown hair on his head. Other than his attempt to hide his baldness, nothing about him stood out. "Check it out," she said to him.

"I swear," I said, my voice wavering. "I was called in after she went missing."

"Missing?"

"From the photo shoot. Everyone thought she hooked up with an assistant or something and left." I paused. "Then I saw her makeup bag and I knew something bad had happened to her. I just knew it. . . ."

"Is that so?"

"*Yes*, it is." I refrained from stomping my foot. "This is all the wrong place at the wrong time. I didn't kill her. I didn't even really know her." I ran a hand along my face. "Even if I knew everything about her, I wouldn't kill her. I don't even kill spiders in my house. I use a glass and take them outside."

"I see," she said, looking me up and down. "Let me ask you a question."

I had thought she was already doing just that but, again, kept my mouth shut. No use antagonizing the cop in charge of solving the case.

"How did you know she was murdered?" she asked.

I blinked. How did I know? She hadn't made a sound as she plummeted through the air. That and the fact that she was missing for the last few days, as well as what Stephi had told me about her sleeping with Jean-Claude. All of which made me suspect the worst.

This was all too surreal. I was standing there, in wet clothes, with vomit on my leather boots, and this cop was basically asking me to confess to murder. "I—" I began.

"Don't say another word." Chase appeared at my side, looking much better than he had the last time I saw him. His face had regained its color, and he looked steady and sober. Then again, Chase was a pro at alcohol consumption. I sometimes worried for him, but never pushed. He needed my support, not nagging, and eventually he'd find his way. I hoped.

"My father is a lawyer. I know about this stuff." Chase whirled to face the cop. "Do you plan to arrest Ms. Lane?"

The detective's lips curved into a sneer. That explained the laugh lines, for I doubted actual humor did. "Not at this time."

"I swear I didn't kill Emily!" This time I couldn't help but slam my boot to the concrete, causing dried vomit to fly off, landing on the concrete between us. This was getting ridiculous. I was exhausted beyond belief. Sick to death about Emily. And I'd reached the point of no return. Any minor push would send me over the edge and straight into hysterics. I fought off a wave of crazed laughter threatening to burst forth.

"It's okay," Chase said, patting my back. I let him for a few seconds before I pulled away. He took my arm, leading me from the detective without another word.

"I suggest you don't leave town, Ms. Lane." Young tipped her head my way. "You either, lawyer boy."

Chase nodded. Together we headed to Emily Cook's bungalow.

Only a few feet from the very place she died.

CHAPTER 13

"I DON'T BELIEVE this," Chase said to me and the LitSquad early the next morning. We all sat in the sunroom of the bungalow, watching the cops collect evidence and the maintenance crew drain the bloody pool. "They forgot the blueberry scones."

I shot him a death glare. My stomach could barely stand the iced coffee in my cup. "Suck it up," I said, sticking my gum to the lid of the cup before taking a drink as tears grew in my eyes. I blinked them away. "A woman is dead. Murdered, if you believe the cops. It's something out of a nightmare."

Chase's face fell, his eyes filling with hurt. "I was trying to lighten the mood. Sorry."

Guilt filled me. I felt as if I'd kicked a puppy. "Why would someone kill her? And where was she for the last couple of days?"

"Maybe someone held her hostage and then killed her when she proved useless." Ryland tapped his lip. "Emily was alive moments before she splashed into the pool. That's for sure."

"What makes you say that?" I asked. "I didn't hear her scream. If she was alive, surely she would've screamed."

"You're right." He nodded, emphasizing his words. "I think someone killed her, and then threw her off the balcony of one of the upper floors." His voice lowered as he stared at his hands. "I saw what looked like handprints around her neck, and her body was still warm when I started CPR."

My hand flew to my throat. I couldn't imagine how it would feel to have someone choke the life out of me. Air refused to fill my lungs for a moment. I took a gulping breath. "That is so horrible. Who would do something like that?"

Just as I said the words, Damien and Dante Grimm walked into view. I had to admit, Damien looked damn good in his Levi's and tight T-shirt, his dark hair shining under the sun. His muscles looked bigger than the day before. My breathing grew harder.

V wiped her chin with a napkin. Probably a coincidence, but still. "Let's meet suspect number one and his twin, suspect number two." She tilted her head, still watching the twins. "Something is up with those two. They show up, supposedly chasing a 'ghost,' and a model from one of their very own ghost-hunting videos ends up dead." She stopped. "I bet the cops should have them arrested by noon."

"Or Loey," Chase said. "The detective had a jones for her."

This time Ryland and V joined in on the death glare I gave Chase. What was wrong with him? Chase didn't appear the least bit upset about a woman flying off the roof. Then again, he hadn't been there when she swan-dived into the water. The memory still gave me the shivers. The terror she must've experienced. Again I rubbed at my throat.

"What?" he asked, his hands in the air. "It's the truth."

I ignored his comment, instead focusing on what V had just said. "What do you mean? Emily was in the twins' video?"

"I thought her name sounded familiar," V said, chewing on her lip. "And then I googled her last night after you went to bed." V fingered her phone, pulling up Emily Cook's wiki page. "She lists an episode of *Ghost Hunting with the Twin Brothers Grimm* under her credits."

I frowned at the image of Emily on her page. Was she the same woman Damien had left with last night? I wasn't sure.

The build was about right, as was the hair color. But a million girls in LA fit that profile.

Could Damien be a killer? The thought sent my stomach rolling. "Do you think the cops know about the twins' relationship to her?" I debated what to do if they didn't. I surely didn't want to talk to Detective Young anytime soon. Then again, Emily deserved justice, nor matter what the cost to me. Justice she might not get unless someone told the cops about Emily's work with the twin Grimms.

And her possibly deeper relationship with Damien.

"We *have* to tell them!" Chase leapt from his seat. "I knew those guys were off. I said it time and again."

Ryland raised one thick but nicely waxed brown eyebrow. "You only hate them because they have more followers than you do."

Chase pulled back, shock and anger etched on his face. "Loey has a ton more followers, and I love her *#YouandMeGirl*. I just don't trust those two."

"He has a point," V said, taking a bite out of a muffin. "It seems like too much of a coincidence to be one. I think we need to call that detective."

Reluctantly I nodded. V and Chase suspected them. And yet something about Damien told me he wouldn't do something so sick. But what about his twin? Maybe he killed her after she left the club with his brother. I pulled out my iPhone, using the speaker so the LitSquad could hear what the detective said.

Chase began vlogging the call. When I shot him a dirty look, he said, "Just in case she tries to trick you into confessing something."

"I have nothing to confess," I said. Or at least nothing I'd tell the detective. My secrets were my own. Not that even one was all that juicy. "Hi, this is Loey Lane, from last night," I said when she answered with a curt "Young."

"Yes, Ms. Lane, what is it I can do for you?"

I swallowed. "I . . . have some information about Emily Cook."

"And?"

"Well . . ." I gathered my courage. "Emily did an episode of *Ghost Hunting with the Twin Brothers Grimm*. Did you know that?"

"Is there a point to this?"

I winced. "The Twins. They're here . . . at the hotel. They arrived yesterday. And I think I saw one of them with her last night . . . before she—"

The detective cut me off. "I'm aware of the Grimms' arrival."

"Oh." I bit my lip. "Do either of them have an alibi?"

"Ms. Lane," she said.

"Yes?"

"Leave the investigating to the professionals." She paused. "Now, is there anything else?"

"No. I guess not." I took a steadying breath.

"I have a question for you," she said. The line crackled, and then her voice rang clear through the static of the phone. "Last night you said you stayed in the victim's bungalow because the hotel was booked. Is that right?"

I frowned, not liking her tone one bit. Suddenly, Chase's vlogging this call made me feel a little better. I made sure to look at his iPhone before I answered. "Yes, that's what happened. Ask the hotel staff."

"We did."

Dread filled me at her tone. "And?"

"According to the registry, the hotel is running at less than half capacity."

The LitSquad gasped.

"How is that possible?" I asked.

"Why don't you tell me?" She stopped, and I could almost feel her smirk through the phone. "If you'd like to come down to the station, I'm sure we can discuss the matter further."

V grabbed the phone, placing the detective on mute. "No way. If she wants to talk, she can come arrest you. You aren't saying another word."

I pressed to unmute. "Sorry, I'm busy for the next couple of days."

Chase mouthed the word *lawyer*, and then rattled off his dad's number.

"You can call my lawyer, though, anytime." I gave her the number and then hung up. I turned to the squad. My eyes filled with tears. "Sounds like Chase was right. Young thinks I did this."

Chase, who was still vlogging to his followers, agreed on camera. I waved for him to shut it down, which he did, with a reluctant frown. "My subscribers are eating this up." His smile grew. "I gained two thousand in the last few hours."

"Good for you," I snarked. "I'm going to look great in an orange jumpsuit."

Chase shook his head. "Not going to happen."

"Why not?"

His smile twisted into a smirk. "Because in LA, the jump-suits are blue. Light blue. To match your eyes."

"Gee." I gave him a deep frown. "Thanks."

"I'm kidding." He lifted his phone. "I'm going to call my dad right now, tell him what's going on. Don't you worry—I am not going to let the cops arrest you."

I felt slightly mollified. "Sorry about being bitchy. I'm just scared."

V patted my hand. "We all are. But none of us are going to let anything bad happen. I promise."

"Thank you." I took a long sip from my iced coffee. "If the cops are focused on me, that means Emily Cook's actual killer is going to get away with her murder."

They agreed with nods.

"We have to do something."

They all nodded again.

"Right now."

"Oh," V said, rising from her seat. "You really want *us* to solve a murder."

I held out my hand. "No one else is going to get justice for her."

Slowly, first Chase, then V, and finally Ryland put their hands on top of mine. "LitSquad," we yelled, raising our hands in a shout.

CHAPTER 14

FOLLOWING OUR BATTLE cry, we broke off into groups of two—V and Ryland in one, of course, and Chase and I together in the other. I didn't really mind. Chase wasn't a bad guy. I think he had a little crush on me too, which didn't hurt.

A girl liked to be liked.

Off Instagram was even better.

Not that we were meant to be.

"What do you want to do first?" Chase asked, his puppy-doggish eyes on mine.

I squirmed a little under his stare. I had no idea where to start. No matter how much he trusted and believed in me,

I didn't have any answers. We needed clues, but where to find them? "I guess we look in her bags? Maybe she left something that will tell us who killed her."

"Like a note? I doubt it's going to be that easy," he said with a grin. When I failed to laugh at his joke and instead gave a small cry, he said, "We don't have to do this, you know. We can leave it to the cops."

How I wanted it to be just that easy. Leaving it to the people who got paid to risk everything felt like a grand idea, until I faced reality. The cops had me in their sights for suspect number one. Until I proved otherwise, they wouldn't search for the real killer. "Do you, like, trust the cops to reveal the killer?" I took his hand, holding it tightly in my own. His skin felt hot, much more so than it should have under the cooling breeze of the air conditioner.

He shook his head.

I dropped his hand, blew out a long breath. Closing and reopening my eyes, I straightened my spine and headed for the bedroom closet, where Emily Cook's lonely belongings sat tucked away. The pink bags looked just as they had a few days before. Sad and alone. Untouched by their owner. Where had Emily gone before her leap off the building? And why?

Could these bright pieces of luggage hold the key to revealing her killer?

I hoped so.

With a deep breath, I started to unzip the first one. The bedroom filled with much too much silence, my breathing and the clicking of each tooth of the zipper on the suitcase the only sounds. My muscles tightened with each notch until they threatened to cramp.

"Boo," Chase said from behind me.

I screamed, jumping a foot in the air.

He laughed, a sound that grated on my last nerve. "Relax, Loey," he said. "The suitcase didn't kill her."

I shot him a withering look. "But it very well might lead to the person who did."

"We already know the answer. Those Brothers Grimm. Who else could it be? I bet the cops already have them under surveillance." He stopped, his voice lowering. "Unless . . ."

"Unless what?"

"No, never mind. It's too crazy."

"What?"

"You know, the rumor."

I closed my eyes. "About the ghost." In unison, we repeated the warning: "*If you see her, you are the next to die.*"

"I'm sorry, Loey. I know how much this upsets you." He brushed his hand over my shoulder. "I wouldn't bring it up, but . . ."

"Emily's dead."

"What if she saw the ghost before you?" He sucked in a breath. "And it killed her like it tried to do to you."

"That's insane talk," I said, sounding tougher than I felt. What I wanted to do was grab my bags and get the heck out of there. But I had to stay. Now more than ever. Emily Cook deserved some kind of justice.

"Is it?" He paused. "Can you explain whatever it was you saw the first night or felt in the pool holding you down?"

Words refused to form on my lips as I pictured the apparition floating, pink mist surrounding her, in the very place Emily landed, barely two nights before. It had looked so real.

And the rumors . . .

Chase frowned. "That's what I thought."

I stuck out my tongue.

An hour later, Emily Cook's belongings were scattered over the bed. After the, dare I say, spirited discussion, we'd gotten back to the business at hand. Somewhere in her belongings, there just might be a clue as to who killed her—real or supernatural.

I pulled out an inexpensive necklace from a jewelry box with obvious signs of wear and tear. I remembered seeing the worn gold pendant in the photo on her wiki page. I peered closer at the tarnished locket. An inscription sat inside. Sadly, the engraving had long disappeared, leaving a vague outline, much like looking through Emily's belongings did for me.

Since her baggage had been a bust, there was only one option left for finding out more about the dead woman and who might've killed her. Though I dreaded doing it nearly as much as I did staying another night in this haunted hotel.

CHAPTER 15

MY HEART SLAMMING in my chest like it did after too much caffeine, I knocked tentatively on the door of room 7744. I felt ill, and not in the good way. The late-night lack of sleep turned my skin green under various foundation and concealer.

When no one answered, I knocked again, louder. The faint sound of whispers from behind the closed door tickled my ears. Someone approached the door. I could feel a dead-eyed stare through the peephole.

"What?" the person barked.

"Um . . . it's Loey," I said.

"Who?"

I sighed. "Loey Lane. We've met a few times now. I'd like to talk."

A long silence ensued. I shifted my weight from one foot to the other. "Are you still there?" I asked, even though I heard more hushed chatter behind the door.

Without notice, the door flew open, and my worst nightmare stood inside: ten stunning models staring at my puffy, slightly greenish face. I swallowed the sudden rush of insecurity. "Hi," I said, putting as much good energy into the one word as possible. My friendliness failed to fly, if the grim-faced June's expression was any indication. I tried again, with a bigger smile. "Can I come in?"

June blew a cloud of vape smoke into my face. She obviously hadn't seen the "No Vaping" sign plastered all over the hotel. "What do you want?" she asked, sucking in another hit of mist that smelled vaguely of jelly beans.

I waved away the toxic mist. "I think we'd be better off if I can come in and we could talk." I didn't want to have this conversation standing in the hallway for anyone or anything to overhear. I didn't need anyone else thinking I was crazy.

"Fine," she said with a shrug, kicking the door wide.

I moved past her and into the room. Apparently the models were sharing the space. Clothes lay all over, some carelessly discarded, while others held places of honor on the table, side lamp, and old-fashioned standing mirror in the corner.

"So what did you want to talk about?" June asked, blowing another cloud of vape in my face.

I stifled the cough. "Emily."

She straightened. "Why? What business is it of yours?"

"She died last night," I began, only to be stopped when she shrugged.

"Yes, we know." She wiped at her eyes as if wiping away tears. Yet her gaze looked fairly dry to me. "Why do you care? You didn't know her."

I exhaled sharply. "That's true. But I was there when she died."

Half of the models gasped. "You killed her?" they yelped in unison.

"No, no. When I said I was there, I meant I saw her hit the water after—"

June stepped in front of the models. "As interesting as this is, we"—she motioned to the women behind her—"need time to mourn her loss." Her eyes fell on me. "So if you'll excuse us . . ."

"Sure, of course. I was just hoping we could compare notes. See if anything stands out about her last few days?"

"Like what?"

"Like the fact you weren't too pleased with Emily."

Her gaze flickered to Stephi, who sat nervously on the bed. "Your source is mistaken."

One of the models raised her hand like the schoolgirl she might very well have been. "Did you talk to her boyfriend?"

Good idea. If I could find him. According to Twitter, most murder victims were a) murdered by someone they knew, or b) killed by people in clown costumes. I thought back to the graveyard and the mysterious leering clown. Goose bumps formed on my arms. I cleared my throat, focusing on the boyfriend. "No. Did she mention him by name?" I asked.

"Nope." The young woman chomped down a piece of gum. "She just referred to him as 'The One.' Like he was all a girl could dream of."

I doubted *The One* would be listed in the Internet phone directory. "Did she say where he lives?"

"Sorry."

"Can you remember anything else about him?"

Again her shoulders lifted, but this time her eyes slid to June. "Jean-Claude was pretty pissed about it."

So on top of blaming Emily for ruining his relationship with June, Jean-Claude was also jealous. A lethal combination. Was that the reason she was dead? I had to find out more about where Jean-Claude was when Emily died. I bit my lip. "Do any of you know Jean-Claude's room number?"

"Room 7754," June said with glee. "Down the corridor and to the right."

I turned to leave, but June's next words stopped me.

"His room faces the pool."

CHAPTER 16

A FEW MINUTES later, I thanked the herd of models and left. Was it possible Jean-Claude, in a fit of jealous rage, had killed Emily? It didn't sound much like him, at least not the man I'd briefly met at the pool. But sometimes you really didn't know people until you checked their Instagram.

I started toward Jean-Claude's room, but that odd pink mist formed, drawing me past his room and up the stairs. I climbed and climbed, my breathing labored. *What am I doing?* I asked myself, unable to stop from following the mist up to the thirteenth floor.

Was this pink mist showing me a clue to Emily's murder?

Or leading me to my very own?

Either way, I couldn't stop climbing to the top floor. Literally. My legs refused to listen to my brain's commands to halt.

As I arrived at the last floor, the mist faded. I opened the door to a flat-topped roof, surprised to find a hot tub and sauna looking out to the Hollywood skyline but no ghost. Or even a scary clown.

With the exception of a few chaise longues and fluffy white towels in standing racks, the space looked empty. I stepped to the railed balcony, my heart in my throat. I looked down into the hollow pool.

My head began to swim.

Was this the last thing Emily saw?

I took a deep breath of smoggy air, proceeding to cough until my lungs hurt. Breathing deeply was frowned upon in the Los Angeles city limits.

"Just the woman I hoped to see," a deep male voice called from behind me. I jumped, nearly toppling over the edge until a strong grip pulled me to safety. "Are you insane?" Damien asked, his fingers still on my waist. "You could've died."

I drew in a sharp breath, annoyed by his high-handedness and the way his grip on my hips made me a little weak in the knees. My skin heated, turning my cheeks red. "Let me go."

He did, but not before he spun me around to face him. "What are you doing up here, alone?" His voice was deeper, darker, than normal. "It's dangerous."

I raised an eyebrow. A look I long ago perfected with the help of eyebrow wax. "What's it to you?" Rather than feel intimidated by being alone on the rooftop where a woman might well have died, with the man who very well could've been her killer, I felt the outrage pulse through me. "What are *you* doing up here?" Was he here to destroy evidence of his or his sibling's crime?

He laughed, with little humor. "I knew it."

"What?"

"You are the one," he said, shaking his head. A lock of hair fell over one eye. I wanted to gel it into place, but I didn't have my purse with my backup hair product inside it.

"I did not kill Emily!" I yelped.

He stepped back. "I never said *you* did."

"Oh." I blinked up at him. "I'm the one what then?"

"You lied to the detective, telling her I left the club with Emily." He paused, his icy stare burning into mine. "Which I didn't."

"Is that so?"

"Dante and I are here for the ghost, not to kill some model I barely knew." A smile flickered on his lips as he leaned in, whispering, "For your information, I prefer my women to be a hell of a lot smarter than to get themselves murdered." How I wanted to believe. It was the way in which his voice oozed sincerity. But I knew better. Damien was far from the honest sort.

The last part of the sentence sunk in. "Are you blaming the victim for her own murder?"

"Absolutely not," he snapped. "I'm *sure* she had no clue she was hanging out with a violent *psycho*."

He did have a point. Not that it was the victim's fault. But putting oneself into dangerous situations wasn't the smartest of moves; things like setting down your drink at a frat party could have life-changing consequences.

Same with standing on rooftops with potential killers.

My eyes narrowed. "How is it you barely knew Emily after she acted in an episode of your show? And I don't use *acted* lightly."

"What's that supposed to mean?" His gaze burned into mine. "Are you saying you don't believe in ghosts? That my videos are fakes?"

I shook my head. "Answer the question."

"You first."

"Fine," I said. "I don't know what I think about spirits. But I surely don't believe in the ability to hunt ghosts. It's an obvious ploy. You're here to gain subscribers."

His hand flew to his heart, and he took an affected step back. "Oh, ouch. I'm so sad a woman who stands around in a bikini all day hasn't fallen for my ghost-hunting—what did you call it?—sham."

When he threw my words back at me, when I heard how they sounded, my cheeks heated. Who was I to judge? "I said *ploy*, but the point's the same," I muttered.

"Now, I'm going to be a gentleman and answer your question." His eyes grew hard on mine. "To start, I sure as hell wasn't with Emily Cook last night. She was on set for a day at the most, so when I say I barely knew her, I mean it. I rarely work with the reenactors. . . ." His voice trailed off as his lips pulled into a frown.

"Who does?"

"No one who would murder a helpless woman and then throw her from the hotel, so you can quit batting your eyelashes up at me." He spun around, his spine ridged as he stormed to the door, throwing it wide. "I suggest you get inside before the person who did harm her returns." He stopped, his voice as cold as a Kansas winter. "And remember, sweetheart, curiosity killed more than the cat."

CHAPTER 17

"HE SAID THAT?" V shook her head a few hours later as we sat down to a nice dinner at the dark, wood-paneled hotel restaurant. From the large window, we could almost see the historic Grauman's Chinese Theatre. But thankfully not the supposed ghost of Victor Kilian, said to haunt its hallways. "How uncool," V finished.

"I know, right?" As I told the squad about the pink mist trail to the thirteenth floor and then my encounter with Damien, I grew more and more irritated. Not only had he tried to intimidate me, but he'd threatened me. I was at least

80 percent sure of it. Even though he'd saved me from top-pling over the edge of the building originally.

But that was before I admitted to bringing the cops to his door, as well as calling his entire livelihood a scam. "What is it with men?" I directed my gaze at Chase, who was picking his teeth with a fork, and then to Ryland—I wasn't sure, but it looked like he was trying to smell his own armpit.

"What?" he said, when he glanced up.

V rolled her eyes with disgust. I suspected Ryland wouldn't be kissing V anytime soon. He must've realized it too, for he gave me an eye roll of his own. "Her loss," he said. "Now what was it you were saying? Did Grimm really threaten you?"

Chase perked up. "For reals? Let's beat his ass."

It was my turn to give an exaggerated eye roll. "Down, boys. I'm positive Damien wasn't threatening to kill me. I think he wanted me to stop looking into Emily's murder, though. Especially at the end." I bit my lip. "I can't figure out why, unless he knows something about her murder."

"Tell us again what he said," Ryland said.

I raised an eyebrow. "Oh, you plan to listen this time?"

He laughed. "I'll do my very best."

"All right." I grinned, launching into my tale from the beginning, leaving out the part about my being a klutz and how good his fingers felt on my waist. "So then he wants me to believe he barely knew Emily. That he didn't leave with her last night. That he wasn't in charge of the reenactments on his channel. When I asked who was, he, like, got all mad, and that's when he said the curiosity-killed-the-cat line."

Ryland snapped his fingers. "Dante."

"What?"

"Dante, his twin, must be the one who worked with Emily." Ryland rubbed his chin, looking satisfied, like a TV detective who just solved a major case.

Before he could say more, a server in a freshly pressed white shirt and black tie came over for our order. I selected a vegetable pasta dish and a white wine. The server looked me over, and I handed him my ID before he could ask. Under all my makeup I still looked in my teens. Not bad when one was over twenty-one, but sure had sucked when I wasn't.

The rest of the squad pulled out their IDs and finished ordering food and drinks. The server left, and we got back to the matter at hand. "It makes sense," I said, pulling on my chin with freshly manicured nails. "Why else would Damien have reacted that way?"

"Because he is a psycho!" Chase said in a voice loud enough to draw the stares of the other diners.

I shot them an apologetic smile before turning back to Chase. "I don't think so," I said.

"Stop thinking with your lady parts," he hissed.

I drew back, shocked.

He winced. "I'm so sorry, Loey-bean. I didn't mean that. It just makes me nuts to think of you at the mercy of that monster. You could have been killed!"

"I appreciate your concern, Chase. I really do." I gave him a wide smile. "But I'm a big girl. And I can handle myself." As much as I wanted to believe that, to be powerful, I was smart enough to admit that when it came to brute strength, Damien could've done whatever he wanted. I couldn't have overpowered him. Which made me think of Emily. Had she fought off her attacker? Or did she go meekly, like a unicorn to the slaughter?

Tears burned the back of my eyes. I blinked them away. Crying for her struggle wouldn't help Emily now. She needed me, it was clear. I would find her killer. And I'd make him pay.

CHAPTER 18

AFTER DINNER, SADNESS set in. I was exhausted, both
mentally and physically. Chase's delightful proposal to stay
in and get massaged while binging on eighties horror flicks
sounded like heaven. V and Ryland opted out, instead disappearing together, hand in hand.

A woman with hands the size of hams rubbed me in various sore spots, especially my poor, battered thighs. I moaned
with pleasure as she worked on the soles of my feet.

"This is the life," Chase said from the massage table next
to me. "I think I'll order up some dessert from room service.
What do you want? Ice cream? Cake?"

"I'm good," I said. I loved food. Pasta, pizza, seafood—I'm in. But sweets weren't my go-to. Give me a nice avocado salad and some sushi anytime. "But feel free to get some for yourself."

Nodding, he rose, naked, from the table as the women finished our massages. I quickly glanced away until he wrapped a robe around his body. He tipped the women, generously, and then headed for the hotel phone.

While he ordered I perused my various social media accounts, posing for a few selfies, which I turned into dazzling art with the help of different filters. I posted these and then moved on to read the comments of my universal LitSquad. My subscribers always made me smile, no matter what was happening in my life.

> @Tiger_Lily: How's the HOT ghost hunter?
>
> @JamieB: New story time, please.
>
> @Big_Ace: Show us your boobs!

Chase came to sit next to me on the couch as I let out a loud sigh. What was up with the pervs on the Internet?

"What's wrong?" he asked.

"Same old, same old." I waved to my iPhone screen.

He nodded. "Living." He turned on a movie with a long-chinned actor fighting with his detached hand. I vaguely recognized the guy from some TV show from my youth. I half-watched the movie while I checked in with my friends all over the world. Once I finished, I hopped over to Emily Cook's IMDb page. It did indeed list the twins' show— episode 124.

I searched YouTube until I found the episode. As the video started, the twins appeared on-screen dressed in ridiculous nightscope goggles and SWAT uniforms. They were at the Winchester Mystery House in California. The crazy, multi-roomed mansion was built by Sarah Winchester. Emily Cook played Sarah in the reenactments. She was dressed in nineteenth-century clothes, but I could still tell it was Emily, even under the heavy makeup used to enhance her age.

The twins showing up here to hunt a ghost and Damien possibly being the last person to see Emily alive were just too much of a coincidence to ignore. What if Emily's "One" was Damien?

I needed to know more about Damien's relationship to Emily, if they had more than a passing one. I started a deep google for Emily, paging through thousands upon thousands of results provided in 0.16 seconds, without finding a single reference to her "One."

Nor a single bit of evidence linking her to the ghost hunter, other than the one video episode.

As I was about to give up, a video clip of Emily from Snapchat caught my attention. It had been uploaded less than twelve hours ago. An hour after Emily left the club with Damien.

And then swan-dived off the thirteenth floor.

My hands shook with the realization that this might very well be her final moments.

Her last testament.

With my heart in my throat, I pressed "play."

CHAPTER 19

I COULDN'T BELIEVE the video that flashed across my screen: Emily Cook, barely recognizable, her hair hanging in tatters around her face, filled my iPhone. Tears fell like rivers from her black, raccooned eyes. Her makeup had washed off under the salty water.

Her fear was palatable through my device. Shivers ran along my spine as she spoke, in broken sentences. *"If you're watching this . . . I'm dead. . . . Oh, God."* More sobbing—deep, raw, and ugly. For a second, she seemed to gain a tiny bit of control, which made her fate that much worse. *"The stories are true."*

What stories? About her and her mystery man? Or the rumors about her one-sided relationship with Jean-Claude, and June's reaction to it?

I soon learned the answer.

But it was far more terrifying than the other options.

"The ghost killed me." More tears silently fell. *"I didn't . . . I saw her . . . two nights ago . . . and then stuff started happening. . . . Weird stuff."*

I pressed "pause" on the video, my hands shaking as oxygen refused to enter my lungs.

"What?" Chase glanced up from the horror movie playing on the sixty-inch television screen hidden in the wall. "What is it?"

Swallowing hard, I motioned to my iPhone, and Emily's frozen, tearstained face. "I found a video. Emily Cook's last one, I think."

"What?" He leapt to his feet. "You're kidding? What does she say? Does she know she's going to die? Who killed her?"

"The ghost," I whispered, my voice hollow. "The same one I saw. Emily saw it a few days before me."

"Loey," Chase said, his face contorting with concern. "You're as white as a sheet." He grabbed my hand. "You can't believe this ghost will kill you too."

I didn't want to believe it. But the proof was in Emily's final moments of terror. "But what if she does?"

"I'm not going to let anything happen to you." His grip tightened, almost painful now. Which was oddly reassuring. "I promise."

"None of us will," V said, appearing in the doorway of the bungalow. "Not that I believe in ghosts."

I looked at Chase and then V, happy to have them by my side. Yet what good would they be against the supernatural? We knew nothing about the spirits. Only what we learned from *Scooby-Doo* reruns. Which equaled out to, the bad guy always got caught by the meddling kids and their dog with a speech impediment. But we didn't have a scrappy dog.

Nor did my friends and I have a clue how to stop a murderous ghost.

I didn't want my LitSquad to get hurt. I loved them. Each and every member, both in-person and online. I wouldn't risk any of them. "Thanks, guys." I gave them a brave, albeit watery smile. "But I think you should leave. Now. Tonight."

"What?" V yelped, her face growing hard as my words sank in. "No way. If you're staying, we are staying."

Chase held up his hand. "I say we all get the hell out of here."

"For once Chase is right." V looked shocked by the admission, even as she said those very words. "We all should get the hell out of here. Someone here is an *actual* killer. Not of the boo variety either."

"I can't leave." My voice sounded foreign to my own ears.

"The *FAS* cover isn't worth your life," V barked.

"No, it's not."

"Good." She reached for my hand. "Let's pack."

"I can't leave, V." I moved back. "Please understand."

She frowned. "When did you get a death wish?"

"Far from it. But who else is going to stop this? I'm the only one who sees the ghost, so unless I do something, she will find some other unsuspecting victim. Maybe even a child. I can't risk it."

"The ghost hunters can handle it," she said. "They live for this stuff."

How I wished it was that easy. The hunters couldn't hunt what they couldn't see or find. My fate was sealed from the moment I'd seen the ghost materialize in front of me.

The thought of my own body lying at the bottom of a bloody pool, much like Emily's had, flickered through my brain. My flesh grew cold, almost as cold as when the pink mist appeared. I swallowed, fearing what would happen next.

Whatever it was, I would face it.

Alone.

As if reading my mind, Chase said, "I'm not going to let you sacrifice yourself." He paused. "What would happen to all the members of the LitSquad without you?"

"This is all too crazy." V paced in front of me, her long legs eating up the space between us. "I still don't believe in ghosts, let alone the fact they can kill."

"Then watch," I said, holding my iPhone out to her. "Emily is *sure* the ghost is going to kill her. And then . . . well, you know what happened to her."

V took the phone, her hand trembling much like my own. She looked at me and then to the screen before pressing "play." Emily's face pixelated and then came into focus. V turned up the sound loud enough that Chase and also Ryland, who had just joined us, could hear Emily's pleas.

"I thought the rumors . . . about the ghost were a prank . . . or a ploy to get guests at the hotel." More sobs. I closed my eyes; the sound of her crying sliced into my brain. I would never be free from the sounds. Not as long as I lived. *"Why didn't I listen?"* she cried into the camera. *"I'm going to die. The ghost is coming for me."*

V paused it, her complexion tinted white.

I swallowed hard, well aware of how she felt. Seeing Emily in such pain, such fear, it was almost too much. "If you pack now you can make the last flight back to Vegas," I said, my voice pleading.

"You. Are. Not. Getting. Rid. Of. Me."

"Don't you see?" I pointed to Emily's tear-streaked face on the screen. "I'm already doomed. But you aren't." I swallowed back a wave of tears at the thought of something terrible happening to my friends. "You have to go. Right now."

After a brief argument—V, Ryland, and Chase on one side, and me on the rational side—the LitSquad, much to my dismay, refused to leave without me, no matter how much I begged. Instead, we watched and rewatched Emily's video for evidence about whoever or whatever had killed her.

Sadly, Emily's last moments held little clue to her murder, except for her very real fear. A fear that haunted me long after I'd gone to bed and turned out the lights.

CHAPTER 20

THE SILK SHEETS felt like heaven against my tired muscles as I relaxed on the fluffy pillows. Sleep didn't come, not for a few hours. When it finally did, I tumbled into a dreamless world. Darkness—for once, my friend.

And then I heard it.

A scream, much like the one I heard the first night, filled my head. My body froze, much like it had when the diving board broke and I fell into the pool. I couldn't move. Could barely suck in a breath.

Seconds later, I jerked awake, finally free. My heart slammed violently in my chest. I looked at the bedside clock.

It blinked 3:14 a.m. With my breathing still coming in shallow gasps, I leapt from the bed, wrapping the soft robe around me in one motion before I ran to the living area.

Chase was sound asleep on the couch. The door to the second bedroom, occupied by V and Ryland, was closed. Had they not heard the scream? Had I dreamt it? I debated waking Chase, but a string of drool hung from his open mouth, indicating a deep sleep. Plus, I wanted to keep him, along with V and Ryland, safe from ghostly harm.

My iPhone lay on the coffee table by Chase's head where I'd dropped it a few hours earlier. Quietly, I slipped it off the glass table and turned it on.

I opened the video camera app on my phone. Normally I used a Sony A500 digital camera for vlogs, but I wasn't about to dig around in the dark until I found it tucked away in one of my bags, not tonight. Furthermore, I wanted real-time comments, so I opted for Twitter, using the live-stream feature.

I turned the camera toward me. "Hey, my beautiful friends," I whispered as I headed for the door to the pool. "As you can see, it's late, and for this follow-me, I'm not my typical self." I motioned to my non-made-up face. It glowed white in the camera light, giving me a ghostly visage. "But I need you all. At the very least to know what happened to me." I swallowed back the bile tickling the back of my raw throat. "Just in case."

I quickly filled them in on what had transpired so far, including the scream that had woken me. "Am I being silly?" I asked. Comments began to pop up under the video.

> @CatFancy01: Have you ever seen a horror movie? Don't go out that door.
> @BigBillyOne: Don't go out there #AnyBlackActorinaHorrorMovie
> @TheOnly: If you don't go, u'll never know. We got u, girrrrl

"Thanks, guys." I grinned, reassured by my online squad. "I'm happy you have my back. Right now, I feel like I don't have a choice. I can either face my doom and get peace for Emily Cook, or hide from it for the rest of my days—or day, depending." My spine straightened. "It's time to find the truth."

Holding the camera up, I opened the door to the poolside. It let out a loud squeak, sounding much like a scream in the silence of the night. But not the scream that woke me. That was different. High-pitched. Almost like a screeching moan.

With tentative but determined steps, I moved through the door and to the still-empty, but at least clean, pool. The streaks of red had been washed away, but the memory of what happened would continue to haunt me forever. Poor Emily. She'd had so much to live for.

Had that been her last thought?

I walked around the pool, to the diving board, still cracked in half from the photo shoot. The very place I saw the spirit days ago. I squinted into the darkness, leveling the camera, and waited.

And waited.

No pink mist appeared.

Relief filled me.

As I turned to leave, lights began to flicker as something like the electrical storm from the first sighting started to form a few feet away. I could almost reach out and touch the energy.

Unlike the last time, no pink mist or female spirit formed.

Just a ball of malevolent violence.

The hair on my arms rose.

Colors swirled. Red. Blue. Silver. Green.

The specter grew stronger, bigger, as the air all but pulsed with energy.

I stepped forward, as in a trace, reaching out, unable to stop myself.

"*Et abiit*," a deep voice yelled from behind me, as what looked like a police baton flew into the center mass of the ghost-light.

The once-growing apparition exploded into a brilliant display of sparks, and then only darkness was left in its place, my stupor vanishing in an instant at the crackle and pop. I jumped a foot into the air. Strong arms wrapped themselves around me, pulling me back off my feet. I struggled in the tight grip, dropping my phone in the process. It hit the ground with a bang, like a gunshot in the now cold silence of the night.

"Hel—" I screamed, but a hand over my mouth cut me off.

I bit down, and my attacker yelped but didn't release me. I lashed out with my foot, but missed my intended target. Rather, my foot connected with his thigh. I pushed off, trying to gain enough leverage so that I could escape.

I tried to scream again, yet this time he stopped me with a few words. "Loey, I'm trying to help you." Damien Grimm quickly dropped his arms, and I fell to the ground. Thankfully my butt hit the concrete first. He winced, offering me his hand.

I refused. Instead I wobbled to my feet under my own power. "Who do you think you are?"

One dark eyebrow shot up, followed by a small grin. "Sorry 'bout that. But next time, don't be so stupid."

"What?!"

"I said, don't be—"

"I heard what you said!" I paced back and forth, trying to rid myself of my growing anger. It didn't work, so I moved faster, adding in a muffled curse every few steps.

He grabbed my arm, pulling me to a stop. My skin under his hand tingled. A side effect of the ghost energy. Nothing more, I assured myself. "You could've gotten yourself killed," he said, voice tight with barely suppressed anger. "That electrical field was enough to curl that hair of yours for good, along with what I'm sure are perfectly manicured toes."

"Pedicured."

"What?"

"Manicures are for your hands." I waved my fingers absent-mindedly. "Pedicures are all about toes."

He snorted. "Fine. Your perfectly pedicured toes. Happy now?"

I shrugged. Happy was far from what I felt at the moment, with his hand still on my skin. He must've realized it, for he let me go. I frowned as he pulled out some sort of odd meter with the same, once-offending hand. It looked like an old iPhone with wires and stuff hanging off of it. "What's that?" I asked, to distract myself from how his hands had made me feel.

He looked down as a green light appeared. "It's a EDI meter."

"Okay," I said, my tone filled with sarcasm. "That makes total sense."

He held out the detector. "It stands for *Environment Detection Instrument.*"

I exaggerated an eye roll. "That helps."

Genuine humor spread over his face. My throat tightened at the beauty of it. "It tracks electromagnetic fields, among other things," he was saying. "I use it to find EMF readings."

"Still not following," I said.

Unlike most men, when I asked a question, he didn't look at me as if I was some dumb blonde. Instead he took his time to explain. "Ghost energy. This helps me find what goes bump in the night. Green means no ghost. Red, well . . ." He held up the meter, showing me the screen. Red lights screamed. "The power that ghost generated is like nothing I've seen."

I shivered, knowing and hating the fact Damien had just saved my life. Worst still, he knew it too. "What was that you said before?" I motioned to the space where the energy had materialized. "To the ghost?"

"I said"—he grinned—"'Be gone.'"

I frowned, recalling his words. They sounded old, and foreign. "It sure didn't sound like it."

"In Latin." He shot me a wink. "Works to banish a ghost about fifty percent of the time."

"Say it again."

He did. Slower. I repeated the phrase. And again. Practicing in case I needed it. He nodded, and then frowned as if he realized why I'd made the request. "I'm not going to let anything bad happen to you, Loey." His eyes held mine. "I promise."

"And that's supposed to make me feel better?" I asked. Damien was good at making promises and then not showing up. "Emily Cook probably heard the same from her *boyfriend*, and we both know what happened there." I emphasized the word *boyfriend*, hoping for a reaction, but his face remained impassive.

He looked me slowly up and down with heated eyes. "Ah, but I'm not your *boyfriend*." His gaze settled on mine. "And my superpower is hunting ghosts. I got this, Loey."

I stared into his eyes, seeing only my reflection. My gaze moved to his lips, so soft yet demanding. . . .

He stepped closer, lifting his finger to trace it along my cheek. "You're playing with fire here." I closed my eyes, thinking he might try and kiss me. Instead of a kiss, he dropped his hand, eyes hot. "Go home before you get burned," he whispered. "Again."

With the word *again* echoing in my head, a reminder of his standing me up last year, I picked up my iPhone and then headed back inside the bungalow. I paused outside the door. "Damien?"

"Yeah?" he all but growled.

"I'll see you in the morning."

"What?"

"You're going to help me hunt this ghost." I stopped, taking a deep breath. "Even if it kills one of us."

CHAPTER 21

THE NEXT MORNING, I woke to find a freshly showered Chase, a fully dressed V, and Ryland, who looked like he hadn't slept a wink, standing at the foot of my bed. I nearly screamed, but threw my hand over my mouth before any sound burst forth.

"So what's first?" V asked, taking a long drink from the white Rockstar can in her hand, which explained her eagerness at such an early hour.

"Breakfast," Chase said, patting his tummy. "I'm *#starving*."

I tilted my head, holding back a loud, unladylike yawn. "It's way too early for hashtags. I'd go for a meme, though."

Chase laughed. "Fine. No hashtags this morning. But a yes to hash browns?"

"All right." I slipped out of the bed, glad to have my friends here with me even while terrified one of them would get hurt if they stayed. After last night's ghostly energy, I knew it was only a matter of time. Someone else would die. I prayed it wouldn't be one of my squad. "We should grab a quick breakfast and then hook up with the twins."

"What?" Chase yelped. "You can't be serious. You want us to team up with them?"

I nodded.

He raised his hand, then let it fall. "I'm against this, Loey. We don't know if one or both of those twins killed Emily. After all, you saw Damien with Emily the night she died." He licked his lips. "It's possible we are all walking into some sort of sick trap."

"I don't think so. Damien doesn't want our partnering with him any more than you do." I turned to V and Ryland. "Do either of you have anything to add?" V shook her head, but her companion nodded. I called on him like a schoolteacher. "Yes, Ryland?"

"Shouldn't we get some ghost repellant or something?"

I grinned. "Think they sell that at Walmart? Or is that more of a Target thing?"

"Funny," he said, deadpan. "But I'm serious. We're walking into something we know nothing about." His voice lowered as if he might be overheard. "I'm with Chase. Are you sure we can trust these guys?"

I pictured Damien's face, the way his eyes stayed on mine as he ordered me around like a jerk. I wanted to say yes, that I trusted them. But the words died on my lips.

I wasn't sure about anything, let alone if we could trust two grown men who chased dead people for a living. But we needed them.

If we had a chance at stopping this ghost . . .

On the other hand, I needed the squad on their toes, and watching their backs in case V was right and the killer was less supernatural and instead much more Grimm. "I don't know," I admitted. "Keep an eye on one another." Unshed tears thickened my voice. "I love you."

"We love you too," they responded in unison.

The sentiment soon faded into tense silence.

CHAPTER 22

BEFORE WE LEFT for breakfast, Jean-Claude called on the hotel house phone. I picked up the line in the bathroom as I decided on a makeup scheme.

"Hi," I began.

Without preamble, he said, "Meet me downstairs, by the Blossom Room, in thirty minutes."

"All right," I said slowly. "Anything in particular I should wear?"

"Black. Wear black," he said, and then hung up.

Black? That was an odd request for fashion shots, but he was the photographer, so I'd do as he asked. *Up to a point,*

I thought, remembering his sloppy attempted seduction at the pool on my first day here.

I dressed in a black baby doll dress and leather boots. Taking care with my makeup, I was about five minutes late in meeting him outside the famed Blossom Room on the main floor of the hotel, the very room that held the first Academy Awards in 1929.

When I arrived, breathing heavily from my half sprint in four-inch heels, Jean-Claude was nowhere in sight. Neither was hide nor pony-colored hair of a single model, production assistant, or bit of camera equipment.

Anxiety tickled my senses. Had I screwed up my shot at the cover by being five minutes late? That seemed ridiculous. Something else was going on. I was almost sure of it. I stood, waiting for twenty minutes.

Still no sign of anyone.

I debated calling Jean-Claude. Would that make him even more angry after my drenching him yesterday? Before I made up my mind, a familiar-looking woman with black hair and a black sheath dress caught my attention.

"Emily?" I called.

It couldn't be.

She was dead.

Was I seeing her ghost?

Should I follow it? Ask it questions? Could ghosts speak without a Ouija board?

The vision opened the door to the ballroom, vanishing inside. I decided to follow, slowly, searching for telltale pink mist. Was I walking into a trap? Was the killer ghost lying in wait?

Inside the beautiful ballroom, the glass ceiling filled the room with soft light. The woman/ghost stood a few feet away, her back to me. "Emily?" I ventured again.

The woman spun around, and I instantly knew two things: I wasn't talking to the ghost of Emily Cook, and Damien hadn't left the club with Emily either. This Emily look-alike was the same woman from the club—Damien's lover, most likely.

Something akin to jealousy filled me.

I willed the feeling away.

Her eyes looked quickly around, as if someone might overhear us. "Can I help you?" she asked slowly.

"I . . . I thought you were . . . someone else."

"No problem," she said with a relieved smile. "How are you enjoying your stay at our Hollywood Roosevelt Hotel?"

Sadly, I couldn't give her the glowing review she obviously desired. "It could be better." I smiled to soften the blow.

"I'm so sorry to hear that." Her face fell. "If there's anything I can do . . ."

Maybe there was. Rumors of the killer ghost had to circulate through the employees. After all, the bartender, Jed, had joked about the ghost. Now that I thought about it, he hadn't been teasing at all. "How long have you worked here . . . ?" I asked.

"Sarah. Please, call me Sarah." She motioned around the ballroom. "It seems like all my life. The hotel has been in my family for generations."

"Then you know the rumor," I said.

Her gaze grew shuttered, and her mouth thinned. "Not sure what you're talking about."

I raised an eyebrow. "Really?"

She held her breath, and then blew it out. "Damn, I hired the ghost hunters GHOULA suggested away from the Knickerbocker hunt to fix this."

Not Damien's lover then. Or at least not yet.

Her answer did explain why the Grimm twins were in California, though. The Knickerbocker Hotel, a visual landmark in the congested skyline, was also said to be haunted by Harry Houdini. Every year for as long as his wife was alive, a séance was performed on Halloween night in hopes of connecting with his ghost. "GHOULA?" I asked. "Who's that?"

"They're not a who, but a what," she answered with a sigh. "It stands for 'Ghost Hunters of Urban Los Angeles,' or something like that. They know all the supernatural players, and said the Grimms were the best around. And we *need* the best."

I had no idea ghost hunters had an actual regional association. I smiled at the Kansas version, GHOUK. Not quite as cool as their LA counterparts. "What makes you say that?"

She frowned, her shoulders falling. "So many odd things have been happening lately. I mean, the Roosevelt has always had its share of 'ghosts.'" Her fingers curled into quotes. "Not as many as the Cecil Hotel, but enough to gain some notoriety. Until now."

I bit my lip, trying to remember what I'd heard about the Cecil Hotel a few miles away. It came to me in a flash. The fifth season of *American Horror Story*, featuring Lady Gaga in all her bloodsucking, fashionista glory, was based on events at the infamous Cecil Hotel. Thankfully *FAS* hadn't booked us there. I could handle one or two ghosts, but I drew the line at vampires.

"Faucets turning on, lights flickering, vacant rooms calling into the switchboard—no problem. Then all this other stuff started happening. A rumor circulated the Internet about a killer ghost, and people started canceling their reservations." Wetness formed in her eyes. She quickly blinked it away. "We're losing money. And if the ghost hunters don't stop this, we'll be bankrupted in a year."

My forehead wrinkled. "So if you have cancellations, why was I told there weren't any rooms available when I checked in?" I asked, biting my lip. Why hadn't they told Detective Young as much, rather than make me look like a liar?

She slowly nodded. "I'm sorry about that. But the bungalow is beautiful, isn't it?"

While it was gorgeous, it was also haunted. That I could've done without. "Yes."

She dipped her head and disappeared into a door at the back of the room. Not really answering my question. I stood there, looking after her.

A cold wind swept over my skin. I turned to the door, but no one had opened it. The icy feel grew until my breath came out in a cloud.

Oh no.

A pink mist swirled around the ballroom floor.

But before the ghost appeared, the ballroom door flew open, and a tall, dark-haired figure stood in it. My heart leapt, and then stilled when I saw it was Dante, not Damien, who'd rescued me from the ghost this time. Not nearly as satisfying.

The meter in his hand screeched so loudly my ears hurt. "Where is she?" he shouted when he saw me.

"Who? Sarah?" I asked.

"No, stupid," he said. "The ghost."

"I don't know."

His eyes narrowed. "Worthless."

Anger burned inside me. Seriously? What was wrong with this guy? His brother was so sweet. Being around the twins was like eating salty and sweet. Sometimes a pleasure, until you had too much. Then you ended up with high blood pressure. "What did you call me?" I growled.

"What are you even doing here?" he asked. "Go back to vlogging about the latest fashion trend. Damien doesn't need the distraction right now. It could very well get him killed."

"I distract him?" I laughed bitterly. "I'm not the one following me around like a lost puppy." Which was more than a bit of an exaggeration. Damien was more like a feral cat. Skittish and sometimes downright dangerous.

Dante snorted. "Don't kid yourself, blonde. Damien isn't sniffing around, hoping for a crumb of affection. He has lines and lines of far better-looking women after him." He frowned. "We both do."

Ouch. Internally I flinched at his sharp words, but I held my head high.

My silence evidently annoyed Dante even more, for he lashed out. "One good thing came out of the horror show in Kansas. You didn't get a chance to get your claws into my brother. Fluff—no substance."

"What?" I asked calmly, my tone belying the rage churning in my gut. I was plenty substantive. Why was Dante so angry with me anyway? What had I done to him, other than practically drool over his twin.

"I said, you're all fluff—"

"Not that," I bit out. "The other thing."

"It doesn't concern you."

"Why do you dislike me so much?" I tilted my head. "What have I ever done to you?"

"Damien's fascination with you affects his work, and that affects me." He pulled at the collar of his shirt, flashing a thin, angry scar on his chest, right above his heart. "See this?"

My eyes narrowed on it, and I swallowed. The pain must've been intense. He was lucky to be alive. "What about it?"

"This happened one year ago, at that bakery." His lips curled with disgust. "In all the years we'd been ghost hunting, neither of us had gotten seriously hurt." I flinched at the implication. But he was far from finished. "Then Damien runs into you, and the next thing we know, this . . . thing . . . like a darkness with no face . . . attacks, nearly killing us both. Had Damien been paying better attention to our equipment . . ."

"I'm so sorry," I began.

"I don't want your sympathy." He took a step toward me, his face cold. "I want you to stay away from my brother. He's already spent a week in a coma because of you."

The realization that Damien hadn't stood me up a year ago, that he'd nearly died, weakened my knees.

Dante wasn't done. "I'm not sure his body would survive another attack like that."

Tears formed in my eyes, but I blinked the wetness away. "I wish I could stay away," I said, and meant it. I didn't want

Damien to die. "But I can't after last night." After last night, I was sure someone else would die unless I stopped this ghost. But I wasn't about to share that information with the angry man in front of me.

"Gross," he said.

I rolled my eyes. "Not that." Well, not that exactly. "Damien asked me to join forces with you to catch the ghost," I lied. He'd done just the opposite, in fact.

Whether the twins were happy about it or not, the LitSquad and the Ghost-Hunting Twin Brothers Grimm would go put an end to this spirit for good.

Or die trying.

The very thought of losing my friends—or Damien, for that matter—terrified me more than chasing a dead woman. My skin prickled with awareness, like death lurked just over my shoulder, waiting for a chance to strike.

CHAPTER 23

AFTER I CALMED down, I headed toward the bungalow. No more ghosts or pink mist appeared, for which I was grateful. For all my outward confidence, I didn't feel even half as much courage when facing the ghost alone.

Would that be my friends' downfall?

I sent a prayer to the heavens to protect them.

Before I reached the pool, I made a quick detour to a house phone to call up to Jean-Claude's room. The phone rang and rang. He never picked up. A polite woman asked if I wanted to leave a message. I declined with a polite thank-you. Jean-Claude had my mobile number if he wanted to be in touch.

Again I wondered about his vanishing act after he asked me to meet. Nothing I could do about my modeling career now.

I opened the door to the bungalow a few minutes later, shocked to see the LitSquad waiting in the hall. Ryland stood, dressed all in black. V only smiled and shook her head when I asked why. "I want to blend in," he declared.

I held back a laugh. "You do know it's daylight. In sunny California. You couldn't stand out more if you tried."

V giggled, but patted Ryland's shoulder. "It's okay, big guy. Come on, I'll buy you a drink after we catch this bitch."

A few minutes later, after I changed into a pair of comfortable capris, a T-shirt, and matching kicks, we found ourselves outside the Grimms' twelfth-floor hotel room, my hand poised to knock on the solid wood door. Before I could it flew inward and Dante Grimm appeared, his face twisted in his trademark grumpy snarl.

At least now I understood a bit of his animosity toward me. Not that it made me feel any better. Dante would continue to hate me no matter what I did. I only hoped he wasn't right. That I wouldn't cost Damien his life.

Without a word to us, Dante turned to his twin, Damien, who stood behind him. "Your girlfriend's here," he barked.

Damien rolled his eyes, ushering us inside their suite, though reluctantly. The room was the same size as the models' room. Two twin beds sat in the center. A flat-screen TV hung on the wall. Lots of open desk space occupied the right side of the room. But it was the window that grabbed my attention.

A large window, surely big enough to fit Emily's body through, opened to the pool below.

Damien cleared his throat, gaining my attention.

Before he could say a word, I said, "Thank you for letting *us* join you on your expedition. You know everyone?"

"Loey, this isn't an expedition." He took an intimidating step forward, all hard muscle and annoyance. "It's a ghost hunt. A very real and dangerous one." He waved to the squad. "Why don't you and your friends stay here while Dante and I work. When it's all over, I'll take you"—he paused, seemingly averse to adding—"*all* to dinner."

Chase laughed, but without humor. "I don't think so. We're in this. You can't stop us from finding the truth about this murderous ghost."

Dante snorted. "Have it your way. But you better keep up. We're not going to stop and wait for any one of you." His eyes lingered on me.

"Now wait a—" I started.

Damien cut me off. "Ignore my brother. He's had a recent breakup. Now he hates all women. I hope it will pass soon, before someone kills him."

"Bite me," Dante said.

"How sad," Chase said, his tone making it clear he could care less about Dante's heartbreak. "So what's first? Do we fumble around until one of your cameras gets lens flare and then you call it a ghost?"

"Play nice," I said to Chase. It would work so much better if we could all get along. I vowed to do just that. Even with Dante's griping and the way Damien looked in his jeans. "Ignore my friend. He doesn't have an excuse for being a jerk."

Snickering, Chase said, "Sure I do. Wealth and breeding. My family came here on the *Mayflower*. Well, not here, in LA, but the East Coast. We didn't like the winters, though." He rubbed his bare arms. "Too cold on our aristocratic skins."

The LitSquad laughed, knowing Chase was joking, at least partly. His family did hail back to the *Mayflower*, but as indentured servants. It was a point of pride in the Tilly family. A genuine rags-to-riches story, even if the riches part came almost two centuries ago.

The Grimm twins did not join in. Instead, Dante and his twin checked and rechecked the equipment scattered over the room—on the beds, the desk, the floor, the full-length mirror covered with a sheet in the corner, everywhere.

Ryland lifted what looked like a baton cheerleaders might toss at football games from a pile of gear on the bed.

Dante grabbed it out of his hand. "Careful, mate. That has a kick." He threw it in the air, catching it on the other end. Suddenly electrical sparks flew from the tip.

The very same tip Ryland had tried to peer into only moments before.

V stepped back, a frown on her sultry, painted lips, as if she just realized how we might be in actual danger. From ourselves. "How dangerous is this? Not that I'm buying into this killer ghost theory, but . . . *it* can't . . . hurt us, can it?"

Dante shot V a nasty smirk. "Why don't we ask that model Emily? Oh, right, she's dead."

"Emily was terrified the ghost would kill her," I said to V before she tore into Dante. Last thing we needed was a blowup between the two groups. The room was tense enough. "And if the rumor is true . . ."

"Right," V said, exhaling a long breath. "Worth a shot if these guys can save your life."

I nodded.

Ryland took the baton from Dante, carefully, so as not to burn his hand. "So where do we start?"

As it turned out, we didn't see a ghost—not yet, anyway.

Instead we witnessed something far more vindictive.

Namely a sober fashion photographer on the run.

As we rode the elevator down to the pool, I checked in with the virtual LitSquad, sharing our ghost-hunting plans on Twitter's live stream. The comments started rolling in seconds after I logged on. "Hey, my loves." I smiled into the camera. "As you can see, Loey's LitSquad has joined forces with @GrimmTwins to hunt this killer ghost."

> @WelcomeMatt: I like ur outfit
>
> @CJ_IS_ME: Get a shot of the ghost hunter's butt
>
> @MissyRead: Was that a ghost flicker over ur
>   shoulder?

The elevator dinged and I stepped off, still intent on the camera. Unfortunately, I ran, literally, into a man carrying two matching black duffel bags. Bags large enough to fit a body inside.

"Watch it," an annoyed Jean-Claude yelled as I smacked into him.

I looked up, surprised to see him, and even more shocked to see his luggage. "Going somewhere?" I asked, all former friendliness gone from my voice. His leaving had my senses on high alert. If he wasn't guilty of something, why was he sneaking out of the hotel before we finished the fashion shoot? And why had he stood me up this morning?

He dropped his bags, throwing his arms wide. "I'm getting the hell out of here. You'd be smart to do the same."

I tilted my head, urging him to speak his mind. "Why is that?"

His face went through various emotions—fear, grief, sadness—stopping on guilt. "Emily, the cover model before you," he said, "the one we thought had left? Well, she didn't. Instead she's dead. Did you know that?"

Maybe we wouldn't have to chase a ghost after all. Jean-Claude looked ready to confess to her murder.

And then he did. Sort of. "It's my fault."

A collective gasp rose from our group.

His eyes widened as if he realized what he said, along with how it sounded. "No, no. I didn't actually kill her, if that's what you're thinking. But it's still my fault she's dead."

"How so?" I asked, not sure I believed his plea of innocence.

"I brought her here." His hand moved to his face. "And now she's"—he gave a small cry—"dead." All anguish left his face, and instead he appeared thoughtful, brows knitted. "She was quite beautiful, on the outside." His gaze focused on my breasts. "Unlike you, Loey. You are as beautiful on the inside as you are on the surface."

I wanted a hot shower just listening to him. Apparently I wasn't the only one disgusted by him, for Damien moved protectively in front of me. "How long were you and Emily involved?" he asked, his voice offering little comfort.

Jean-Claude pulled back. "We weren't. I didn't . . . Who told you that?"

"Does it matter? It's true, right?" I asked quietly. I didn't want to throw Stephi under the proverbial bus. One bad word from Jean-Claude and Stephi's career could be over.

"Oh, God." His shoulders slumped. "What's the point now? Yes, Emily and I had a fling. If you could call it that."

"What *else* would you call it?" Damien asked.

"Photographer with benefits," I said, repeating the words Stephi had used.

Jean-Claude's eyes burned with anger. So much so, I stepped back, running up against the hard muscle of Damien's chest. "I was the reason Emily had a career at all," Jean-Claude said. "*FAS* wanted another model for the cover, but I insisted we use Emily instead. And how did she repay me? She ruined everything!"

I rubbed my tongue across my teeth. Would losing the cover spot be enough of a motive to kill? "Who did *FAS* originally want for the cover?" I asked.

He frowned. "The young one. What's her name?"

"Stephi?"

"Yeah, her," he said. "But she wasn't ready for a cover yet. Too inexperienced."

Or, far more likely, she wouldn't put out.

"This isn't helping anything." Dante pushed between us. "Can we get back to hunting this ghost before someone else winds up at the bottom of the pool?"

"In a second," I said. "Jean-Claude, when was the last time you saw Emily?"

"A few days ago." He picked up his bags. "When she told June about our sleeping together."

"You didn't see her after that?" I asked. "Didn't confront her? After all, she ruined your relationship with June. Weren't you angry?"

"Of course I was." He lowered his voice. "I went to her bungalow about an hour later to talk to her, but she was already gone."

My eyes narrowed. I knew he was lying. Don't ask me how, but I just knew it.

"Come on, Loey. We aren't getting the answers we need here," Damien said, ushering me past the photographer. I glanced back in time to see the smallest of smiles flicker over Jean-Claude's lips.

CHAPTER 24

GHOST HUNTING WASN'T like I thought it would be.

On TV and the Internet, it looked like an easy gig. You stood around, calling to the dead, while nightscope goggles and special cameras flared with ghostly energy.

Not so in real life.

We spent hours measuring some electromagnetic fields around the pool. Or something like that. To tell the truth, the LitSquad and I spent most of the time under the warm Cali sun narrowing down the list of suspects to Jean-Claude, June, or a malevolent dead woman.

V and Ryland voted for Jean-Claude after our encounter at the elevator.

Chase went with the evil spirit.

I wasn't so sure.

Of anything, really.

I knew what I saw. Knew the terror in Emily's final video, and her belief in a supernatural stalker. Then again, Emily had slept with June's man. Was that enough to kill for? And what about Stephi? She seemed like an unlikely killer, but Emily had taken her shot at the cover.

While I weighed each suspect, I glanced at Damien's tight abs as he wiped beads of sweat from his face with the bottom of his T-shirt. Damien's eye caught my roaming ones. The side of his mouth lifted into a wicked grin.

Dante cleared his throat loudly.

"What?" I snapped when Dante shot me a death glare.

Damien's attention returned to his equipment setup. He explained the technical stuff in great detail as he worked. Not having a science background, it took me a minute, but then I grasped the basic premise, which was fairly simple. If the EMF device in his palm warbled, then some sort of energy was near, and a bunch of fancy gadgets would determine just what sort of energy.

His plan was to catch the ghost using even more techie stuff.

"Get anything?" I asked, trying to focus on the hunt instead of the way his shirt inched up.

He shook the EMF reader like a Polaroid picture. "Not yet. We might have to wait for nightfall."

"Yay!" Chase held up a drink he'd recently ordered from the poolside bar. "I take it all back. Ghost hunting is awesome."

Dante shut him up with a look.

"Tough crowd," Chase whispered under his breath, which had Dante's face twisting with greater anger.

"What if we break into groups and search the entire hotel?" I asked before bloodshed commenced.

As if he understood my underlying intent and couldn't care less, Damien paired us off: Damien and me, Ryland and V, and the odd couple, Chase and Dante. Neither of them looked pleased by the pairing.

To keep my friends as safe as possible, I said, "Why don't V and Ryland take the first two floors. Chase and Dante can take the next two, and Damien and I will take the rest."

The deadly upper floors.

I swallowed a wave of fear.

"But—" Chase tried to argue, but I cut him off.

"I'll be fine," I said.

"Yes," Dante drawled, in a voice hot enough to melt the polar ice caps, pre–global warming. "My brother will take *good* care of her."

Chase's mouth slammed shut. He shook his head, walking away.

After his twin's heated look, Dante grabbed his ghost-hunting equipment and ran after Chase.

"Can I get one of those EMF readers?" Ryland said, looking excited by the idea of hunting a ghost with V on his arm. V didn't look nearly as thrilled. But boys would be boys.

Damien grabbed one from his bag. He quickly showed Ryland how to use it. "If it starts screaming, call me on this," he said, handing Ryland a walkie-talkie as well.

I raised an eyebrow. "Have you heard of cell phones?"

"Funny," Damien said. "But magnetic fields can screw cell signals. Better to be safe. Use the walkie." He nodded to Ryland. "If Dante or I don't respond, get the hell out of there. Got it?"

Ryland grinned. "This is gonna be fun."

V rolled her eyes. "Yeah, tons of fun." She shot me a wink, lowering her voice so the guys didn't overhear. "For Loey at least."

"What's that supposed to mean?" I asked, though I knew perfectly well.

She nodded toward Damien, who was bending over to show Ryland some techie tool. "That," V said. "Right there is what I mean. You dig him and he can't take his eyes off you."

"You're wrong," I lied. "We're just . . ."

"Just what?"

"Shut up," I said, turning on my heel and walking away from her much-too-seeing eyes.

Her knowing laughter rang in my ears long after we'd parted.

CHAPTER 25

I LOCKED EYES on my iPhone and scrolled through comments from my LitSquad, who were tagging along from home for the ghost hunt.

> @ShaneP: Did you look under the bed? Ghosts
>   always hide under the bed
> @MissyRead: Was that a glitch? I swore I saw
>   something odd at 7.5
> @DavidHas: What color panties are you wearing?

Admittedly, I was being a coward, keeping my eyes on my phone rather than the guy hunting the ghost plotting to murder me. But it was easier this way. For every time I glanced at Damien, my heartbeat increased, my face grew red, and my palms sprouted sweat like a teenager's. Not a good look, for sure.

On the seventh floor, as we stepped off the elevator, the EMF reader went from a calm green to extremely red in a flash. I yelped and jumped back, nearly dropping my phone. Damien handled the change much better, for he let out the smallest of gasps and then rushed forward into danger.

A dumb move, as far as I was concerned.

"Stay here," he said, motioning me back without even looking my way.

He waved the device around, stepped forward, and then brandished it in the air again. I had no idea what he was looking at, as the device stayed red, not moving in either direction.

An odd sensation had the hairs rising on the back of my neck, like a tickle, but not in the good way. It was almost as if something were gathering all the energy from around us. Like a fire grabbing at oxygen. The fillings in my teeth, of which I had two, began to buzz as if I were running foil across them.

A trick I'd learned in elementary school.

Every fiber in me suggested I not turn around.

Unable to stop myself, I did the clearly ignorant thing and slowly, ever so, turned, my iPhone capturing every moment. The light fixtures along the darkened corridor began to flicker. And in front of me grew a cloud of crackling energy, much like it had the night before. Yet again, without the pink, misty warning.

It swirled faster and faster.

As did my head. I felt weak-kneed and faint.

"Duck," Damien yelled from behind me.

I did.

Just in time too.

The electrical entity exploded in a whirl of burning sparks as Damien shoved the baton Ryland had nearly fried himself with into the center mass. At the same time, he grabbed my arm, pulling me to safety as the embers singed the walls. A few fell on his bare arm, scorching his skin. He gasped but otherwise didn't make a sound.

"Oh no," I said, grabbing his limb. Deep, angry burns already blistered his flesh. "Are you all right? We should get you to the ER."

He pulled away, rolling down his sleeve to cover the injury. "Comes with the job. I'm fine. Really," he added, when I started to argue.

The smoking carpet ignited, flames flickering a foot tall. Damien slammed his boot against the burning floor, sending up waves of black, choking smoke. My lungs rebelled, and I started coughing. I held my T-shirt over my mouth until the smoke cleared.

"It didn't have any mist," I choked out a few minutes later.

"What?" Damien frowned, looking around the burnt hallway. "What do you mean?"

"The mist," I said, motioning around our feet. "It wasn't there again."

He gripped my shoulder. "Loey, I need to ask you a very important question."

"Okay."

"Was that . . . thing the same energy you saw the first night?"

"Kind of," I said, unable to explain in words the differences between the two in terms of energies. "I saw it . . . first, and then the pink mist and woman—they seemed, almost, to overpower it." Shivers racked my body as I remembered my terror.

Without another word, he pulled me to his strong chest. My head fit perfectly against him. I wanted to hug him harder, to disappear inside the comfort he offered.

"Can we stop the ghost?" I asked.

"Yes," he said, kissing the top of my head.

"Are you lying to make me feel better?"

He laughed. "Saw through that, huh?"

I nodded against his chest.

"I have to be honest here. I've never encountered an energy quite like it." He paused, tilting his head. "It was almost too intense."

"It was coming straight at me." I pulled away to look into his eyes. "You saved my life. Again."

His lips curved into a smile. "I did—"

A scream drowned his words. I jumped, hitting him in the chin. Damien stumbled backward, smashing into the wall. Painted plaster rained down around us. "I'm so sorry," I started, but he waved me off as a second scream echoed along the corridor. "Stay right behind me," he said, and dashed toward the noise.

I had no choice but to follow.

Or get juiced by . . . whatever it was that just tried to kill us.

I ran after him, nearly colliding with his broad back when he jerked to a stop. Another scream. This one coming from the door in front of us.

Room 7744.

The models' room.

"Stay back!" a woman yelled from inside.

Instead of a polite knock, Damien kicked in the door. Wood splintered as it flew off its hinges, landing on the floor.

More screams joined the first.

"Where is it?" Damien barked, taking control of the situation.

His answer: more screams from the array of half-dressed women inside the room.

I noticed a few, upon seeing Damien in his ghost hunter glory, actually dropped whatever towel or other items of clothing they had used to cover up. Damien didn't seem to notice. His entire attention was on the mirror at the back of the room.

It was the same old-fashioned cheval mirror with bronze accents I had in my room.

The same kind in Damien's suite too.

I frowned, thinking of the thin bedsheets covering the mirror in the twins' room. At the time, I'd thought the guys were just messy. But what if Damien had a greater reason, like keeping the ghost at bay?

Pink mist churned.

An image of a woman in a long white dress filled the reflective surface. Her dress flew up around her, and she used her hand to stop its journey, just like Marilyn Monroe had in her iconic photo from *The Seven Year Itch.*

"Oh my God," I said, stepping closer to the mirror, unable to believe my eyes. "Marilyn Monroe's ghost wants me dead?"

Damien grabbed my arm before I made contact with the mirror. Marilyn's ghost, manifested in the glass, appeared incredibly sad. Her lips were pulled into a tight frown, and her eyes kept looking down. As if she were looking at a specific item causing her pain. Her mouth opened, but like before, no sound emerged.

And then, as soon as she appeared, she vanished and the shiny surface returned to normal.

I turned to Damien, who still held my arm. "OMG, did you see . . . ?"

"Yes."

"That was Marilyn Monroe, wasn't it?"

"She's the ghost we're here for," he said, ripping a sheet off the nearest bed. He threw it over the mirror. "Legend is, Marilyn stayed at the poolside bungalow, the same one you're in, so often that she purchased her own antique mirror. When she died, the hotel packed the mirror away."

My throat ached at the suffering Marilyn must've been in to take her life.

"Years later, during a remodeling, some employee discovered the mirror and placed it in one of the rooms. That's when bizarre things started to happen. People reported seeing Marilyn in the mirror. Items moved around the room at will. The faucets in the bathroom turned on and off. That sort of thing." He frowned, his eyes on the mirrored surface. "But something changed. She's appeared to you at least twice now in other mirrors. And once, at least, outside her mirrored portal."

"That's what the sheet's for? To keep her from manifesting again?"

He shrugged. "Works about ninety percent of the time."

"The ghost will come back?" a model behind me screeched.

He ignored her shouts, focusing on me. "I don't know what that other . . . thing is." He paused. "Or how to stop it." His hand squeezed my arm. "Yet."

Two ghosts.

One a killer. One a famous icon.

How was that even possible? And why were they so different in form?

Damien's face hardened. "All of you need to get out of here. Now," he said to the half-dressed models around the room. "You too," he said, pointing at me. "Your ghost hunt is over."

"Get out of the room?" a ginger-haired model asked.

He shook his head. "The hotel. Hell, LA."

"What about June?" she said, tears filling her eyes. "We can't just leave her."

The models all started talking at once.

He held up his hand for quiet. "Where is June?"

"Dunno," another of the models said, this one wearing nothing but a thong and a sports bra. "She was here. The lights went out. And when they came back on she was gone."

"Like Emily," Stephi whispered.

"What?" I yelled. "You said you didn't see Emily after she went missing."

The model winced. "She was here, talking to June. Then she just vanished."

"Why didn't you tell me before?"

"I wasn't supposed to tell you."

"Why not?" I asked.

"Dunno."

Damien looked ready to kill someone. "Did you tell the cops this?"

The models shook their collective heads.

"Who told you not to tell me?" I asked Stephi.

She looked to her friends, and then back at me. "June."

CHAPTER 26

"D TWO TO D one," Dante's voice called over the walkie, as Damien searched the models' now-vacant room. I had refused to leave with them, even though Damien had all but begged. "Loey, I don't want you to get hurt," he said.

"Same," came my response.

Exasperated, he went back to his gadgets while I stood around, feeling useless. The only thing I could and would do was watch his back.

"D two, go ahead," Damien responded.

"We've got a little problem," Dante said through the crackle of static.

"Oh, I think it's bigger than a little one," his twin answered, his eyes on mine.

"Say again?"

"Never mind." He pressed the "talk" button again. "What's your issue?"

Dante hesitated. "Is Loey still with you?"

"Affirmative."

"Um," he said. "She's not going to like this."

I snatched the device from Damien's hand. "What?"

Silence.

Then the walkie hissed in my hand. "I kinda . . . lost your friend," he said, his tone not nearly as apologetic as it should've been.

"What. Do. You. Mean. You. Lost. Chase?"

A pause. "He was here one minute. The lights flickered and died. And then he was gone."

Damien pulled the walkie from my tight grip. "Where?" he asked.

"Fourth floor."

"On the way," he said. Without looking at me, he gathered up his equipment and left the room. I stood there, steaming both with anger and fear. Chase had to be okay. Had to be. Damien popped his head back in the doorway. "You coming?"

"Do you promise I can kill your brother?" I asked, only half-joking, because if anything bad happened to Chase . . .

Damien shook his head. "But I'll give you one free shot."

I clenched my fists. "Fair enough."

Together, Damien and I ran down the hall and stairs to the floors below, where a still-uncaring Dante stood, a EMF reader in hand. His partner, Chase, gone.

No sooner had we reached him when a crackle of electricity filled the air behind us.

"Here we go again." I looked at Damien, and held up my iPhone so my online LitSquad could watch what very well might be my last moments.

CHAPTER 27

LUCKY FOR US, the electrical storm dissipated on its own before electrifying anyone. The lights did go on and off, though—along with my cell signal, as Damien said it might. The live feed dropped, but that wasn't my greatest concern. Not now.

I grabbed the walkie from Damien. "Ryland? V? You guys okay?"

No response.

I tried again, my heart in my throat.

"V? Please respond."

Damien took the walkie from my shaking hand. "Take it easy, Loey. I'm sure they're fine."

"What if . . ." I trailed off, horrified by the possibilities.

"Loey!" Chase's voice came, slurred, over the walkie. "Is that you? I miss you! Why don't we ever hang out anymore?"

I grabbed the device from Damien. "Chase? You're okay?"

"Course," came his garbled reply.

"Where are Ryland and V? How did you get their walkie?" I asked, then added, "And where the hell are you? You scared me to death!"

He hiccuped into the phone. "Aw, I'm sooorry. Don't be mad, K?"

"I'm not angry. I was worried." I took my finger off the "talk" button. "He's drunk," I said to the twins.

They both raised an eyebrow. Opposite ones, so it looked like one person raising both. Creepy, to say the least. "Duh," both said at the same time, which was odder than the raised eyebrow.

I pressed the "talk" button again. "Are Ryland and V with you?"

The pop of static on the walkie-talkie bounced around the room.

"Chase? Are you still there?"

"Loey! Hi, bae! You should totally come down here and party!" Chase said, as if the last few minutes of our conversation never happened. "I ran into your buddy. The photo dude." His voice lowered to a hushed whisper. "That guy is a little on the weird side, but cool. First he says he's leaving the hotel, and then he's at the bar, buying me drinks." A loud belch followed.

"Chase," I said in my sternest voice. The one I reserved for yelling at my furbaby Riley, when he tried to chew on his little sister. "Where are Ryland and V?"

"Back at the bungalow," he said. "They finished with that ridiculous search for the boogeyman and, well, you know."

"Ridiculous?" Dante yelped. "I'll show him—"

"Quiet," Damien said. "Find out what happened. How he managed to disappear and then end up drunk at a bar."

I asked just that.

Chase responded with, "Disappear?"

He started giggling uncontrollably until I snapped his name: "Chase!"

"I told that guy, the angry one who has zero sense of humor, that I was going. Not that he paid any attention. He was far too busy frowning and muttering under his breath." His voice lowered to a loud whisper. "I don't think he likes you much, Loey-luv."

Damien shot his brother a death glare. Dante merely rolled his eyes.

Chase sighed. "My feet hurt, and I was beyond bored searching for the ghost. Did you know gin and tonic glows blue under the sun? I'm watching my drink glow like a freaking Smurf. It's *epic*. . . ."

Dante's forehead wrinkled, but surprisingly he didn't comment.

"Are you at the poolside bar, then?" I asked.

"Are you coming to keep me company, Loey-bug?"

I blushed at his use of my nickname. Not that I was embarrassed by it—more so his use of it in front of Damien. I did *not* want Damien to start using it. It was too personal. Too intimate. I wasn't sure about my feelings for him, or more important, his for me. As much as I struggled against it, I could feel myself slipping deeper and deeper into real feelings for the ghost hunter.

"Loey? I miss you," Chase repeated.

"I'll be down in a little bit." I paused, thinking about June. "Don't go anywhere. With anyone. Do you hear me? And tell V and Ryland the same. Got it?"

"Ten-four," he said, which prompted another round of giggles.

I handed the walkie to Damien. "Thank you," I whispered. He nodded.

"So what did you find upstairs?" Dante asked his twin. "Because I didn't find crap on these floors. Not even a cold spot."

Damien held up his hand. "Loey," he said. "Why don't you go down to the bar with Chase? Dante and I need to check into that mirror in the models' room." He stopped, his lips turned downward. "Better yet, why don't you collect your friends and leave the hotel until we figure this out."

"Not going to happen." My hands went to my rounded hips. "We need to find June."

"You don't think I know that?" His face went all hard and gorgeous. I pressed my stomach, warding off the butterflies tickling it. Blowing out a harsh breath, he said in an exasperated tone, "Why do you think I want you out of here?"

My forehead wrinkled. "I don't understand."

"I don't think we're dealing with just a ghost. Or even two ghosts, for that matter."

"What?" Dante yelled. "What are you talking about?"

"What does that mean?" I echoed.

Dante and I looked at each other, realizing for the first time, we were on the same side. By the look on his face, he wasn't happy about it. That made two of us.

His better-looking twin's rigid gaze met mine. "If what your drunk friend said is true, and Jean-Claude didn't leave the hotel . . ."

I gasped, drawing back. "Then he might just be behind Emily's murder, instead of the ghosts."

"And June's disappearance." He closed and then slowly opened his eyes. "And more than likely, her murder, if Dante and I don't find her in time."

"You have to save her."

"You can count on it"—he paused, voice husky—"Loey-bug."

CHAPTER 28

I GLANCED AT my cell phone for the tenth time since I'd left the twins, with Damien promising to call when he located June. A drunken Chase, now much to his dismay drinking coffee, sat at the table next to me.

The sun, through the windows of the bungalow, kissed my shoulders, warming the coldness blanketing me. Coldness that had started when Damien shoved me onto the elevator twenty minutes ago. He pressed the ground-floor button before I could argue. To make matters worse, he emphasized his demand for the LitSquad to leave the hotel with a hot, astonishing kiss before the elevator doors closed.

The kiss had been one straight out of a romance novel. The kind where the hero kisses the heroine senseless, and then she stupidly does whatever he wants.

But not this time.

I wasn't going to leave while a woman was missing and a maniac roamed the hotel. Jean-Claude was one smart albeit deadly man. According to Chase, Jean-Claude had plied him with enough gin to fill a number of bathtubs. Oddly enough, during Prohibition, Errol Flynn had used the barbershop of this very hotel to create his own gin.

Unwittingly, a drunken Chase had given Jean-Claude plenty of information about our investigation, such as it was. Starting with: we suspected him of murder.

Or at least he was one of a shrinking list of suspects.

Right up until he admitted to Chase he had wanted Emily dead.

And how June too had broken his heart.

And then he vowed to break hers right back.

Shivers ran up my spine as Chase replayed their conversation. Lucky for us, Chase, even wasted, had perfect recall. To him it was a curse, never forgetting whatever anyone said. No matter how intoxicated. I thought it ran more along the lines of a superpower. I, of course, couldn't remember my own mobile number.

Fear threatened when I realized how much danger Chase had been in. He'd sat across from a killer. A man who'd tossed the woman he'd claimed to love from a rooftop. I could only imagine what he would do with a rich kid from Beverly Hills. Thankfully, other than his belly full of booze, Chase appeared no worse for wear.

"Loey," Chase said, his face green under his tan. "I think I'm going to be sick."

Strike that. A little worse.

I leapt up, helping him to his feet. He ran to the restroom. Retching sounds soon followed. I swallowed the bile rising in the back of my own throat. As the heaves grew louder, I headed to the pool, yellow tape still flapping in the breeze.

Covering my eyes with my darkest sunglasses, I tried to forget about Emily's murder only a few feet away and instead enjoy the sun on my skin, skin already turning a touch red under the rays. *Poor Chase,* I thought, as the sound of another violent round of gin and tonics rose from inside him.

My fingers brushed my lips, and Damien's kiss came back to mind. It had been so short. But so brutal to my senses. I'd barely managed to keep my feet. For a second, I wondered what was more dangerous for me—the hot ghost hunter or the ghosts he hunted.

Rather than ponder the question, I pulled my phone out and tweeted that very question to my followers.

@WickedOne111: The ghost hunter, for sure. Take
a bite.

@888888Boobs: Show me your boobs!

@URMine4Ever: Loey's not afraid of no ghost
hunter.

"Thanks, my beautiful friends," I typed into the phone. A loud bleep from my pocket reminded me that I'd grabbed Chase's phone off the bar when I half-carried him back to the bungalow. I'd forgotten to give it back. Not that he needed it, judging by the continuous sounds of retching from inside the bungalow bathroom.

The phone buzzed again.

I pulled it from the pocket of my capris. Of course, Chase had the latest and greatest iPhone model, plated in gold. Real gold. The phone cost as much as my car. Using his standard 1234 passcode, I unlocked his phone and swiped at the screen to see the notifications.

A Snapchat video had just uploaded.

Normally I wouldn't have paid the slightest attention, but the video came from a familiar account. I blinked as the postage-size image of a tear-streaked woman appeared.

I checked the account name again.

This was the very same one that had posted Emily Cook's last video.

My heart in my throat, I clicked on the image. The video started to play. June's face appeared, eyes red from crying. Her lips were swollen, cracked, and bloody. Whatever had happened to her, it was far from good.

She let out a sob. *"He's crazy,"* she said in a harsh whisper. *"He's going to kill me."*

More uncontrolled sobbing ensued.

The video flickered, and June's face reappeared on-screen. Her tears had stopped. This time she had a new message. One that shook me to the core. She looked dead into the camera. *"And then he's going to kill you, Loey Lane."*

The video went black, her words ringing in the air.

CHAPTER 29

I DEBATED TELLING the LitSquad about the video, fearing their reaction. We had to find June before Jean-Claude finished his deadly mission. If I showed the squad the video, they would insist we leave the hotel. Right now. Heck, if Damien saw it, he would drag me to the airport himself.

But that wouldn't save June.

And it wouldn't give Emily justice.

"What'd I miss?" Chase staggered from the bungalow. He looked a little better, though he was far from steady on his feet. One look at me and his gait steadied and his face sobered. "What? What happened? Are you all right?"

Wordlessly, I held up his iPhone with June's face still front and center. He watched it, the greenish pallor returning full force at her final warning. "OMG, we have to get you out of here right now!" he yelled. "I won't let Jean-Claude get you."

Before I could respond, my Twitter, YouTube, Facebook, and Snapchat blew up. My virtual LitSquad was concerned after seeing the video appear online. I had so many messages I had to turn off my notifications.

> @Giirrrll9: Love.
>
> @HersheyKisses: Call the cops. 4reals.
>
> @ClarkKent: Stay safe.

I bit my lip. The swollen tissue reminded me of Damien. I wondered if he'd seen the video. Or better yet, if he'd found June. I grabbed the walkie from the coffee table in the bungalow where Chase had left it. "Damien? Are you there?" I asked into the static.

Silence.

"Dante?"

Again, more nothing.

A chill ran up my spine. Had Jean-Claude realized Damien was searching for June and . . . "Damien!" I yelled, louder, as if somehow the mere decibel level would save him from whatever evil fate Jean-Claude had dreamt up.

Chase's phone, still gripped in my hand, buzzed to life again. I dreaded whatever might materialize virtually. With a heavy heart, I gazed at the smudged screen. This time a black-and-white video, like those from a surveillance camera, popped up.

A swirl of electricity circled the Grimm twins.

The energy grew closer and closer, backing the twins into a corner. The only protection was the mirror to their side. An old cheval mirror with brass finishings. The same mirror I'd seen the ghost of Marilyn Monroe in less than an hour ago.

Dante screamed as the swirl touched him, sending his body into convulsions.

He dropped to the ground like a stone.

Damien tried to ward it off. He mouthed soundless words.

And then the force threw him into a wall. He fell to the ground, and the camera pulled close on his face. His eyes—glassy and wide, as if all the beauty and life had been sucked out of him.

Then the video went black.

CHAPTER 30

I DASHED TO the elevator, and up to room 7744. I threw open the door and stopped dead.

The room was empty.

The mirror gone.

The only thing left inside was the lingering scent of burnt flesh.

"Damien?" I shouted as tears streamed down my cheeks. "Dante?" What happened to them? I glanced at Chase's phone, still clutched in my hand. The video had been uploaded less than a minute ago. How could they have vanished in sixty seconds?

The answer came to me as the door behind me slammed shut with brutal force.

The video was a fake.

A clever ploy to get me alone.

And I'd fallen for it.

I slowly turned to face my own murder.

Only to find the room still empty. I grabbed for the door, surprised when it opened with little force. What was going on? Should I call the cops? Would they come in time? I remembered Detective Young's disdain, and my long wait for the LAPD on the night Emily died.

Did June have that long?

Did Damien?

I swallowed, knowing what I had to do. Taking my iPhone, I loaded the YouNow app as a hazy plan to delay their suffering at Jean-Claude's hands formed in my head.

Not the best of plans, but one that just might work nevertheless.

Blowing out a harsh breath, I started to record. "Hello, my lovelies. I have to share this with you." I looked dead into the camera—into the eyes of a killer, I hoped. "I know where there is evidence against Emily's killer. Follow along."

I entered the elevator, pressing number thirteen under the watchful gaze of my worldwide squad.

CHAPTER 31

BREATHLESSLY, I HURRIED from the elevator to the safety of the bungalow to call Detective Young. I smiled at the trap I'd cleverly set. Jean-Claude had to follow my every move on social media. He knew too much not to be cyber-stalking me. Therefore, I decided, for once, to use it to my advantage.

I'd set my iPhone on the elevator railing, pressing number thirteen on the console.

Everyone watching would think I was headed up to the top floor.

The killer was sure to follow in real time.

Hopefully that would buy enough time for the cops to come and catch the killer.

It wasn't a bad plan, if I do say so myself.

I opened the door to the bungalow, surprised to see Chase sprawled on the sofa. "Chase?" I called.

He didn't answer.

Was he hurt? Or had the gin and tonics finally worked their alcoholic magic, knocking him out?

Or worse?

My heart leapt into my throat. Was he breathing? I couldn't tell. *Oh God, Chase.* Obviously Jean-Claude had used the video to lure me from the bungalow and Chase, the only witness to his confession.

"Chase?" I said louder, taking a few more steps toward the couch. "Please answer me."

When I was less than a foot away his eyes popped open.

I jumped back in surprise, my hand going to my throat. When I recovered sufficiently, I slowly looked him over for bullet wounds or blood. "You're okay?"

Instead of answering my question, he surprised me by asking one of his own. "Do you really think your trap would work?"

"Yes." I tilted my head. "But how'd you know it was a trap?"

In one fluid motion, he leapt from the couch. I took a quick step back as his body invaded my personal space. Standing this close, I could smell the minty scent of mouthwash on his breath.

Without a hint of alcohol.

Before I could ask why, he grabbed my arm, his fingers digging in. The blood under my skin pooled into a bruise. Anger flashed through me. "Stop," I yelped. "You're hurting me."

"Poor precious Loey." His tone conveyed all the sincerity of a politician. His grip tightened even more, causing me to whimper. "I'll admit," he said with a creepy smile, "when you said there was evidence on the thirteenth floor, and you were going to collect it, well, I almost fell for it." His smirk widened. "Almost."

CHAPTER 32

"WHAT?!" I TRIED to pull away, but he held tight. "No, Chase, not you. I don't believe it."

"Oh, yes, me." Using his free hand, he pulled a gun from his pocket. Of course, the damn thing was plated with gold. Only the best for this madman. He pointed it at my chest. Dead center. "Let's go somewhere a little more private and finish our chat," he said.

"No." I yanked at my arm, hoping against hope to free myself from his brutal grip.

He cocked the revolver.

"Then again"—I stilled in an instant—"I'd love to take a walk."

His laughter sounded like the typical mad scientist's. More of a cackle than a laugh. Had his laugh always sounded so evil? So cold? "Not as dumb as you look," he said with a smile. "But I already knew that."

I ignored his insult. Heck, I'd heard much worse from guys not planning to kill me. Instead, I focused on talking him out of my impending and outright murder. Keep them talking— that's what all the TV shows advised. Though this was far from make-believe. "Why, Chase? Why are you doing this?" I asked.

He chortled again. "This isn't an episode of *Scooby-Doo*. I'm not about to admit to my wicked plan, wrapping everything in a tidy bow while you stall until someone saves you." His giggle grew louder. "Because, let's face it, nobody's coming. You, brilliantly, sent them all to the thirteenth floor." He signaled with the gun toward the door. "Now move it before I'm forced to stain this lovely white carpet red."

I stepped slowly to the door, the gun occasionally tapping my spine. Each step felt like lead weights around my feet. "Move it," he whispered, jabbing the weapon into my kidney. I tried not to cry out, but a whimper escaped my lips.

Could this really be happening? Chase, a bad guy? But he was a rich kid with his every wish catered to him.

Oh, right.

I cleared my throat. "Chase," I began, my tone calm and even. "This is no way to get love from your absentee father."

He nudged me hard in the organ. "Good God, you are annoying. How did I keep from killing you sooner?" he said as we entered the hotel. He pressed the call button for the elevator. When it arrived, we entered, and he pressed number twelve on the console.

We rode up in semi-silence as I plotted a way to escape, while he—I'm just guessing here—plotted a way to dispose of my body. I preferred cremation, but I doubted he was all that interested in my preferences.

A Muzak version of a Justin Bieber song Chase hated filled the elevator as we rose, floor after floor, to my certain death. Unconsciously, I tapped my foot nervously along to the beat.

"Stop tapping or I will shoot you right here, right now." He snorted when I stopped. "Good choice." He smirked. "Did you stop because you believe there is a chance Damien Grimm can come to poor little Loey's rescue?"

I shrugged.

He laughed, again with that maniacal edge I was growing to despise. "Sorry to burst your bubble, but dreamboat can't save you." He stopped, flashing even, too-white teeth. "Any more than he could save himself."

"What?"

"That's right. Damien's dead." More crazy laughter. It bounced off the enclosed space, echoing in my ears. "My very fake but still very deadly electrified 'ghost'"—he curled his fingers into quotes—"killed him."

CHAPTER 33

THE ELEVATOR DINGED, announcing our arrival to the twelfth floor as he finished his confession of murdering Damien. Unable to stop the tears spilling down my cheeks, I said, "You won't get away with this."

He snorted. "I already have. Now move."

The doors opened and Chase stuffed a key card in my hand before motioning me forward.

Had he really killed Damien? How much more blood, including my own, would be spilled today? I only hoped he hadn't hurt V or Ryland. I quietly posed the question as we stepped from the elevator.

"Not yet," he said. He waved to the left, indicating I should head that way.

Relief filled me. My friends were safe.

"Of course," he said, "if you don't play along with my every wish, I can fix that."

I swallowed, hard.

"We're almost there, Loey." He grabbed my shoulder, pulling me to a stop outside a neatly labeled suite. "Room twelve hundred. Fitting, right?"

I frowned, not wanting to annoy the crazy man with a gun. "Fitting? How so?"

Chase sighed. "*The Shining.*"

"What about it?"

"It's a classic. We watched it the other night. After *Evil Dead*. Remember?"

"Um," I said. "Sure. 'Here's Johnny' and all that. But what's twelve hundred have to do with it?"

He blinked. "That's the same hotel room number."

"No, it's not."

"What?"

"The Stanley Hotel—it only has four floors."

"I hate you," he said.

"I understand the feeling." I glared at him from over my shoulder. "I really, really do."

"Unlock the door," he said, jamming the weapon in my back again. For a second I considered refusing. Who knew what he had in store inside that room. Would I be the next to fall to my death? "Now," he added. "Unless you want to see V and Ryland bleed."

I crammed the card into the lock. The light on top went from red to green, and the lock disengaged, loudly. The "Do Not Disturb" sign fell to the ground as I opened the door.

The room was dark, the shades drawn. Two twin beds sat in the center. Empty. In fact, the whole room looked empty. No clothes strewn anywhere. No causally tossed room service trays either. Odd, considering Chase had never cleaned up after himself in his privileged life.

The only item of note was a lone rubber clown mask on the bed.

A shiver ran over me. The creepy clown at the graveyard wasn't some random creep, but Chase in disguise. Had he wanted to scare me?

A thump sounded from the bathroom, pulling me from my thoughts. Before I could question him about the noise, he shoved me inside the empty room, slamming the door behind me. I stumbled, falling to the floor. My leg took the brunt of the impact. Pain ripped through me like a knife. I tried not to yelp, but failed. My knee began to swell under my capris. Soon

I wouldn't be able to walk, let alone run away to save myself. Doom crept closer.

He grabbed my hair, yanking me to my feet. I yelped. "Ow. Ow. Ow."

"Quit whining," he said, smacking me in the face with an open palm.

Genuine rage exploded inside me, dashing all fear I'd once felt. I drew back to return the favor but stopped in time. I needed to stall, not enrage him more. Surely someone would've noticed my absence on the floor above and alerted the authorities.

Another thud sounded from the bathroom.

"Is someone in there?" I asked, once the haze of rage faded from my vision.

He snorted. "If you're so inquisitive, why don't you open it?" He motioned with the weapon to the bathroom door.

The rational, logical side of me said no freaking way was I going to open that door. I didn't want to see what it held.

Not even a little.

But my curiosity, the same cat-killing kind Damien had warned me about, took control. It had to see behind the door. Had to know the truth, no matter how ugly or, in this case, deadly.

Fighting myself, I did as he said, opening the door.

Duct-taped together on the toilet sat Jean-Claude and June. Neither looked particularly happy to see me. Or to be there, for that matter. I tried not to take offense. For a rescue party, I was sadly lacking in skills. And the gun at my back couldn't be reassuring.

CHAPTER 34

UNABLE TO DO anything more, I gave my fellow captives what I hoped was a reassuring smile. Muffled . . . what sounded a lot like cursing . . . came from underneath their taped mouths. Again, I tried not to take it personally. I turned to Chase, his gun leveled at my chest. "So what now?" I asked.

"Well, Loey," he said slowly, "I shoot June there." He gave her a small wave with the weapon. She screamed under her gag. "Then I shoot you."

"But—"

He shrugged. "Sorry about that, but you just couldn't leave things alone."

I frowned as his words penetrated my fear. "Are you seriously blaming me for your psychotic behavior?"

"I am not crazy," he said, biting out each syllable.

"What I don't get is, why?" I tilted my head. "What is it you gain?"

"What do you think?"

Honestly I had no idea. He was rich enough to buy almost anything. So why the ghost ruse? And why kill Emily?

He turned the gun to the side, gangster style. "Know how many subscribers I gained this week alone?" Before I could answer, he said, "Almost a hundred thousand."

"That many," I said with sarcasm.

"You see, I'm smarter than most vloggers," he said. "I knew I'd get a ton of subscribers wanting to see a 'real' ghost."

People wanted to believe in life after death, sometimes desperately so.

"And who better to star in my play than Loey Lane?" He frowned, seemingly lost in his explanation. "It was a perfect plan. No one needed to get hurt. Then Emily goes and makes me kill her. All she had to do was stand on the ledge of the thirteenth floor and scream like the ghost had pushed her off." He tapped the gun to his teeth. Unfortunately, it didn't fire. "All on video, of course," he added. "When she balked, I sort of lost it."

"You didn't have to kill her."

He went on as if I hadn't spoken. "Everything was riding on this haunting. I didn't mean for her to die. I just wanted her to do what I said." He paused, shaking his head. "Once she landed in the pool everything went to hell. You wouldn't leave. No matter how many times I tried to make you." A vein pulsed on the side of his head. "Then your ghost hunter goes and saves you, when it was supposed to be me, on video, who does so."

I bit my lip. The electrical swirl by the pool. Chase had been asleep on the couch, or so I'd thought. He'd somehow managed to create the electrical storm, but Damien had appeared, ruining his plan. I smiled at the thought. For who knows what would've happened had Chase saved me.

I winced as I pictured me in his arms. The entire story would have a very different ending had Damien not arrived. "But why, Chase?" I asked, pleading with the man I knew as a friend inside this new killer persona. "What reason could you possibly have for all of this?"

"Weren't you listening? . . . FAME." A smile flickered over his face, reminding me of my friend. It quickly faded, replaced with someone I very much didn't want to know.

I tried not to let fear clog my throat. "So your bright idea was to stage a haunting? Seems like a lot of work, especially the pink mist."

"Mist? What mist?" He shook his head. "Never mind. Yes, it was work. A lot of work. But worth it."

"Tell me about it," I said, slowly stepping into the bedroom, away from Jean-Claude and June.

Chase followed, the gun hanging loosely in his grip. "Don't humor me, Loey. I am not crazy. And you're far from a psychiatrist."

"Okay," I said, twisting my hand for the best vantage. "But I am fascinated by your plan. How did you accomplish faking an entire haunting?"

"First, I started a rumor about this phantom ghost. Wasn't hard either. I just used the old legend the hotel already had. Updated it for today's culture. I used the idea from *The Ring*. Saying once you saw the ghost, you would be the next to die. Soon the hashtag *#Next2Die* was trending." He stopped, his eyes hard on mine. "What I needed next was a dupe to play my lead role."

"I take it that's me?"

"If the dupe fits." He giggled. "I'd already hired the models and Jean-Claude. The only one left to get on board was you. I called you, saying I was an art director working for *FAS*. You jumped at the chance to fulfill your dream to be on the cover of the magazine. Just like Emily, June, and Stephi. All of you would do anything for the cover, even die."

"I should've recognized your voice," I said, realizing he'd used my ego against me.

His smile grew. "In your defense, I used a voice changer to disguise my voice. You can get an app on your iPhone. Imagine that."

"I'm sure it will come in real handy," I said with a glare.

"Oh, Loey." A giggle, much like that of the old Chase, burst from his lips. "I'm not done amazing you yet. When you arrived at the hotel, I paid the manager to tell you the hotel was full and only Emily's bungalow was an option, since I'd already rigged the poolside 'electric ghost.'"

"All very impressive," I lied, licking my lips. "Then you had me see a ghost the first night?"

"That was the beauty of it," he said. "I had the bartender implant the rumor into your pretty little head, and less than eight hours later you're tweeting everyone the gory details." His giggles grew. "I didn't have to do anything but show up to save the day. On camera, of course."

"Except you didn't save me." I smiled. "On or off camera. Damien did." For a moment, tears blinded me. Damien was trying to help, and I'd gotten him killed by my psychotic *former* friend. I tilted my head as my tears dried. "How could I have been so stupid not to see it? All you ever wanted from me was subscribers."

"I wouldn't have said no to a relationship, but since last year, you only had eyes for that ghost hunter. Too bad too."

A shiver of revulsion flickered over my clammy skin. "So what now? You can't kill all of us. Someone will figure it out, and you'll spend the rest of your days in prison."

His face broke into a wide grin. "Not gonna happen. I do have a plan, you see. I just need to make it look like you tried to save June, but Jean-Claude had a gun." He aimed the weapon at me and then moved it to June. "Jean-Claude shoots the two of you, and then turns the gun on himself." He chewed on his lip as if lost in thought. "What do you say, Loey-bug. How will that play on your channel?" Smiling, he added, "Of course, I'll grieve appropriately."

"Sure you will."

"On camera, of course."

My own smile grew as I played the last ace in my proverbial deck. "Funny you mention being on the camera." I lifted the cell phone from the place I'd hidden it behind my leg. "Smile pretty."

His gaze narrowed on the device and his own crazy reflection in it. "You left your phone on the elevator. . . . How . . . I don't . . ."

"It's your phone." I paused to gloat, just a little. "And millions of people just watched you confess to killing Emily and threaten to kill me. I suggest you run now. Fast as you can."

He looked at the gold-plated phone, and back at me, then to the camera again.

With each eye movement his face grew harder.

I swallowed. Maybe I should've kept quiet. For he wasn't running off, trying to save himself. Instead he looked thoroughly pissed. More so than I'd ever seen him.

Yep. Pissing off the guy with a gun wasn't my smartest move.

"You bitch," he finally uttered.

And then he did run.

Just not away as I'd wanted. Rather, he ran right for me, his hand curled as if ready to choke the life out of me as he had Emily.

I let out a bloodcurdling scream, dropping my lifeline: Chase's iPhone.

CHAPTER 35

PINK MIST SWIRLED around me, growing more and more dense as seconds ticked away. Chase froze as Marilyn materialized in front of me. Her outline grew firmer until she appeared almost human, except for the pink mist, which now obscured me from Chase.

He let out a screech.

Footsteps pounded closer to me.

I tried to run.

A scream, much like the one I'd heard the first night, rocketed through the space. This time I recognized it as Chase's. A full second later, he landed face-first on the carpet in front of me. The pink mist and Marilyn vanished in a wink, leaving me with an unconscious Chase, a strip of carpet wrapped around one of his feet.

Ten seconds later the hotel room door crashed in. I looked up, surprised to see Damien filling the doorway. Pieces of the shattered door rained down around him. "Loey?" he asked, looking more shocked at what he saw than I was that he was alive.

And I was pretty damned shocked.

Relief and joy filled me. Damien was alive!

The video of Damien being electrified by the "ghost" Chase had created was obviously a fake. Now that I thought about it, the wall Damien had crashed into looked a lot like that of the bakery in Kansas. Chase had doctored the video, imposing the mirror into surveillance video from last year. Had I paid closer attention, I would've figured it out before I'd let a lunatic kidnap and attempt to murder me.

I glanced down at Chase. A stream of blood dripped down his face.

"Loey? Are you okay?" Damien asked, concern thickening his voice.

I blinked. "He tried to kill me."

Damien nodded, slowly. "We know. V, Ryland, and I watched the video feed. As soon as he gave the hotel room number, we were on our way. But we ran into some trouble."

He swallowed deeply. "When the feed went black . . . I thought he'd killed you."

I ignored the last part of his comment. "Trouble?"

"Another electrical 'ghost.'" He held up a palm-size device. "He had these set up all over, using large magnetics and power sources, to fry us with 'ghost' energy."

"Jerk."

"V's still freaked out."

"Why? The ghost energy was a fake."

He grinned. "True. But Marilyn's ghost stopped it before it could do us any harm."

I shared his smile. Poor V.

"Last we saw on the feed, Chase was coming at you." He waved to the phone I'd dropped. "What happened?"

I shrugged. "I told everyone I could take care of myself."

He raised a dark eyebrow, a bigger smile hovering loosely on his lips.

"Fine," I said. "Marilyn's ghost saved me too. When Chase ran at me, pink mist swelled. It must've blinded him, for he got tangled in a section of worn carpet." I relived his perfect karmic retribution. "He hit his head on the edge of the exposed bed frame, knocking him out."

"Good." The warm grin on his face eased the coldness lingering inside me. He grabbed me around the waist, lifting me off my injured knee, and headed for the door.

I stopped him before we reached the exit. "What are you going to do about Marilyn's ghost?"

"For starters, I'm going to thank her. But not right this minute. Right now I'm going to do what I've wanted to do for over a year now." Then he leaned down to kiss me.

This time our kiss was far from sweet.

His fingers burned a path down my neck as the kiss deepened. My brain turned to mush. I wanted more. More of what, I couldn't say. His body, sure, but something more too. Something that words couldn't quite express.

As abruptly as it started, he broke the kiss, his gaze burning me in place. "Any further questions?"

CHAPTER 36

I STILL COULDN'T believe the lengths Chase had gone to gain more followers.

Sadly, at last look, his channel had over two million fans.

My LitSquad was extremely active following my near death. Far more of them wanted to know about that kiss Damien had given me than Chase and his fake haunting.

@SMOOTH74: Hubba Hubba

@UR1: Get it, girl.

@EEEWWW: Loey Loves Damien

A still-shaken V kissed my cheek good-bye the next morning. "You probably won't hear from me for a while," she said. "I can't wrap my head around the fact ghosts exist."

"Oh, V . . ."

"Tell Ryland good-bye for me," she whispered.

"Why don't you—"

"I can't." She rubbed her arms as if cold, even under the seventy-degree heat. "Please, Loey?"

I agreed reluctantly.

"Thank you." She squeezed my shoulders. Before I could say more, she motioned to Damien, who was coming up behind me. "Take care of her," she said to him.

He nodded, and then V was gone.

Just like Marilyn, without the puff of pink mist.

A short while later, Damien and Dante finished their hunt, freeing Marilyn from her earthly bonds by shattering the mirror in suite 1200, while saying an incantation in a bizarre language no one but them understood.

As she faded, her once-soundless voice declared, "Thank you."

Yet it was me who owed her a debt of gratitude I could never repay. She'd saved me, and my friends, from certain death. I would never be able to thank her spirit enough.

In her honor, I took a dozen pink roses to her tomb.

Unknown to me, Jean-Claude had shot some candids of the moment. The photographs were quite lovely, gratitude and grief in a moment of quiet reflection. He'd quickly submitted them to an online magazine. Last look, the number of views hung around a million.

Jean-Claude had found his cover shot.

And I a new career.

CHAPTER 37

FOLLOWING MARILYN'S DEPARTURE, the Ghost-Hunting Twin Brothers Grimm had pronounced the Hollywood Roosevelt was ghost-free.

A declaration, apparently, Montgomery Clift's ghost in room 928 wasn't too thrilled about. For he made his displeasure known that night with a trumpet blast every hour on the hour all night long. The remaining hotel guests had quickly checked out. I could almost hear Sarah, the hotel's owner, crying as her revenue departed in their nightclothes.

The boys had plenty more work to do in order to get their payday.

Or so Damien had said, in a terse note I found under the bungalow door explaining why he couldn't see me off.

He vowed to be in touch.

CHAPTER 38

MY PLANE LANDED at Manhattan Regional that afternoon. The bright, crisp Kansas sun, shining through the plane window, worked wonders on my outlook, which, up until that moment, had been less than sunny.

An hour after my plane landed, the Uber pulled to the curb outside my house. The excited bark of my furbabies welcomed me home. I smiled, hoisting my bags from the trunk as I hobbled on my bad knee. The pain wasn't too bad this morning, but enough to remind me of the dangers of psychotic friendships and spooky ghosts.

Before I could open my door, a shiver of supernatural awareness rippled through me.

I glanced up in time to see the lone outline of a figure at the end of my driveway.

A lone, faceless figure like the one Dante said had fried the twins at the bakery last year.

"Who . . . ?" I stammered.

I never got the full question out.

The figure's form flickered and then vanished, leaving me alone.

Very alone.

The slight sound of malevolent laughter in my ears.

ACKNOWLEDGEMENTS

THIS BOOK IS also dedicated to my father, Mark, who listened to my excited ramblings and plans for this novel, but left this earth before he got to see the final version. When I was younger and I would write stories on my clunky, slow-processing laptop, he would sneak onto it when I wasn't looking and write notes of encouragement. Thank you for feeding my hungry soul with music and art and encouraging me to create my own. I am who I am because of you.

Thank you to my brother and creative partner, Christian, for countless nights of no sleep and too much coffee while helping me write this book. Everything in this life is more fun when I have you by my side. Thank you to my mom, Ed, and my entire family for your constant support and patience in all that I do. Thank you to my manager at Select Management Group, Jake Webb, and a special thank-you to Adaptive Studios and StyleHaul for this incredible and unbelievably fun opportunity.